NOBODY TOLD KING PETTY WHAT TO DO

King Petty stared moodily at the ceiling of the Black Bull Saloon. He had an open bottle of whiskey on the table in front of him. The girls that were usually on his lap were keeping their distance, as were his men.

Petty couldn't stop thinking about the widow Brandom, and he couldn't stop thinking about how easily the stranger, Sam Two-Wolves, had taken her from him. Petty was used to getting whatever he wanted, whenever he wanted, from whoever he wanted.

On the other hand, King Petty was bored; Two-Wolves might make his life a little more interesting.

But there was no way anyone could get away with humiliating King Petty; nobody told King Petty what to do—or what not to do.

King Petty decided to make Sam Two-Wolves watch him rape the widow Brandom before he died.

WILLIAM W. JOHNSTONE

BLOOD BOND

DEATH IN SNAKE CREEK

ZEBRA BOOKS
KENSINGTON PUBLISHING CORP.

ZEBRA BOOKS are published by

Kensington Publishing Corp.
850 Third Avenue
New York, NY 10022

First Printing: December, 1994

Printed in the United States of America

Chapter 1

King Petty had no particular place to be and was in no particular hurry to get there. For all practical purposes, he ruled the town of Snake Creek, Texas, and the entire surrounding area. The few men who had dared to defy him had been buried a long time ago. The ones left alive were scared to death of him, including Richard Holt, the town marshal. There was not a man or woman alive who would argue with anything that Petty wanted.

He was involved in a variety of illegal operations, including cattle rustling, that gave him all the money he needed. His men could handle most of that work on their own. He had all the free booze and women he wanted at the saloons in town. Most days, he didn't even have to ask. All he had to do was step through the batwing doors and he found a drink in his hand and a woman on his lap. At twenty-three, he faced no major challenges, no major problems, and he barely knew what to do with himself. He almost wished for the days when men would face him in the street for an old-fashioned shoot-out, just for something different.

Though the morning was bright and full of promise, Petty paid little attention to the weather. He rode aimlessly through the countryside, passing the occasional homestead and scowling. He had contempt for the homesteaders as being weak and inferior, trying to make a poor living out of the hard ground, but otherwise the sodbusters meant nothing to him since they had nothing he wanted. In his mind, even the women weren't pretty. Once in a while he or his men would beat up a farmer or two in town, just for sport; but most of the time the homesteaders cut a wide path around him, and Petty let them go their own way.

Petty reached the top of a small hill and looked down across a field being plowed by a farmer and his team. His young son was working with him, helping to clear brush. Though it was only early morning, the two had already broken a heavy sweat, soaking their shirts. In the distance was a modest farmhouse. The outlaw laughed at the flowers that made a tiny splotch of color by the door.

He spit and said with a sneer, "Sodbusters."

Normally, he would have just kept riding, but something told him to keep his place and continue to view the scene. Petty held the horse steady as he watched, though he became impatient easily. He was about ready to ride away, when the door to the cabin opened. A young woman stepped out, paused with her face raised to the sun.

The woman caught Petty's eye. She was as shapely as some of the saloon beauties that he was familiar with, but wore a simple dress that made her more appealing. Her long hair was tied up on her head. Petty's eyes followed her as she walked to the well near the house, pulled out the bucket, and started toward the field where the farmer was plowing.

The morning suddenly seemed a lot more interesting.

Petty rode slowly, following the woman. The farmer took the bucket. He and the boy each took a drink and wiped their mouths on their sleeves. The man kissed the woman and motioned to the boy. She picked up the bucket and started back to the cabin, followed by her son.

The outlaw let the woman and boy walk out of sight before he nudged his horse forward to where the farmer had already started his plowing again. The man was concentrating so much on his work that he didn't even notice Petty until the horse was almost in the field.

"Hello, stranger," the farmer said. "Can I help you?"

"Maybe. Maybe not." The farmer was a little older than Petty, but not by much. He wasn't wearing a gun, and no gun was in sight. Petty shifted in his saddle to put his own revolver within easy reach. The farmer apparently didn't suspect trouble. He remained standing, hands still on the plow. Petty continued, "You own this place?"

"Working on it."

"That your wife?"

The farmer placed the plow handles to the ground. "What's it to you?"

"Good-looking woman."

"I don't think I like this talk. You just keep on riding."

Petty loosened the gun in his holster.

"You telling me what to do? If I were you, I'd think twice before trying to boss King Petty."

The farmer narrowed his eyes.

"I've heard of you around town. Never thought to see you out here. Would you kindly move on? I've work to do."

"There. You did it again. Trying to tell me what to do. Now you've made me mad."

The farmer took a step back, looked around him. He had no weapon and no path of escape.

"Now, listen, Petty, I have no argument with you. I meant no harm."

"By damned, now you're whining. Now you really made me mad."

He pulled his gun, aimed, and shot without another word. The bullet hit the farmer in the shoulder. He fell to the ground, blood soaking his shirt. The farmer looked down at the blood in disbelief.

"What'd you do that for?" he asked.

"I felt like it," Petty said. "I can do anything I want." His voice was conversational as he asked, "What's your name?"

"Jack Brandom."

"Good. I sometimes like to know the names of the men I'm killing."

He shot again, this time putting the bullet between the farmer's eyes.

Lilly Brandom was now carrying the bucket of water back from the field despite her son's offer to help. Tommy was ten, almost a man, but Lilly didn't mind him being a child just a little longer. He had worked hard in the field and still had plenty of chores waiting for him when he got back to the cabin. She could handle the water on her own.

Life on the homestead was tough, but it was the only life she knew. Her husband was a good provider, and she was loyal to him. She was proud of her son. She would not complain. Life was good, and unless something terrible happened, it would continue to be good.

Lilly even whistled softly as she walked.

She stopped in shock when she heard the first shot. Tommy also froze, then started to run toward the field where he had left his father.

"No, Tommy. Don't go back."

"But Daddy may need help!"

"Go to the cabin."

"No. We need to . . ."

"Do as I say. Run to the cabin and get the rifle. I'll see what's going on. Now go!"

The boy took off, running faster than he had ever gone before.

Then the second shot was fired, and Lilly felt a sinking in her heart. Jack seldom had a gun with him. He didn't like guns, and didn't want having one on him to worry about. So the shots were fired by another. Perhaps it was just somebody target shooting, she told herself. Or perhaps somebody was shooting snakes, since there were plenty in the area.

Lilly ran back toward the field, but was blocked in midstride by a young man on horseback. Beyond him she could see her husband's body on the ground in the field. She couldn't see clearly, but knew he was dead.

"Your husband had a little accident," Petty said.

"Got in the way of a bullet. A shame. Looked like a worker."

"You shot him. You killed him."

"No argument there. He made me mad. And he had something I want."

"You want this land? You don't look like no farmer."

"It's you I want."

Lilly put her hand to her mouth in surprise. She felt nauseous and wanted to get away. She was as trapped in the open as if she had been locked in a room.

"What do you want with me? That you'd kill my husband for?"

Petty laughed. "Old Jack must not have been much of a lover if you have to ask me that!" He rubbed the stubble on his chin. "But I've had enough fun for one day. I'll be coming back for you, my pretty widow Brandom."

"You can't get away with this. I'll tell the marshal. He'll see you hang."

The outlaw shook his head and laughed. "You don't get to town very often, do you? Widow, you have a lot to learn. And I'll be the one to teach you. I think that'd be a lot more fun than I've had in a while with the girls in town."

"Come back here, and I'll kill you. I have a gun."

"Yes, you will be fun! Widow, I'll be back. Anytime I feel like it. As many times as I feel like it. And there's not a damned thing you or anybody else can do about it."

Petty started to trot his horse back to town and was almost out of sight when Tommy returned with the rifle. He saw the body on the ground, and the tears in his mother's eyes.

"What do we do now, Mom?" he asked.

"First thing we have to do is bury . . ." Lilly said, but couldn't finish the sentence.

Tommy was ten years old, almost a man. He returned to the cabin to get a shovel. His father had taught him not to cry. He would let the hurt come out later, when he was alone.

Matt Bodine and Sam Two-Wolves rode leisurely north. The dry country they had seen farther south in Texas had now given way to grass and trees. Sam took a deep breath and said loudly, "This is more like home! There's something about a warm spring morning that makes a heart glad!"

"Yeah, if your heart gets any gladder, you'll be bursting out in song. I'm not sure the world is ready for *your* singing!"

"I can carry a tune with the best of them. When I was in school back east, I was even a member of the glee club!"

"You mean that everybody was filled with glee when you stopped singing?"

"No, my singing was so beautiful that it brought joy to the hearts of all that heard me. Look it up. It's in the record books. That beats your record of spending two days and nights in the San Antonio jail."

"At least they didn't arrest me for my singing!" Matt said, laughing. "It was for that fight after calling out the crooked card dealer. How was I to know he was the sheriff's brother-in-law?"

Sam shook his head. "It did take a little convincing to get them to let you go, but again I saved your butt." He paused. "Hey, I don't think you ever did properly thank me for that."

"I've listened to you gloat about it ever since that time . . . as well as listening to your singing. That ought to be worth something! Just do me a favor . . . don't sing while we're fishing. I'd hate to scare all the fish away!"

Sam paused, scratched his chin, and said, "Who knows? My bright voice might call the fish to us."

The two men laughed as they rode and exchanged their mock insults. The talk was good-natured, because the two men were closer than friends, closer even than brothers. Matt and Sam had not just travelled many long miles together; they were blood brothers in the Cheyenne tradition.

Sam was the son of a great and highly respected Cheyenne chief and a beautiful and educated white woman from the East. Though from different cultures, the two had fallen in love and married in a Christian ceremony. Matt, the son of a rancher, met Sam when they were both kids. The two quickly became friends, with Matt spending as much time in the Cheyenne camp as his ranch home, and Matt was adopted into the tribe as a True Human Being, according to Cheyenne belief. Matt and Sam were joined by a ritual of knife and fire.

In many ways, they appeared similar and were often mistaken for brothers. Both were young, in their early twenties, handsome and muscular, over six feet tall and weighing over two hundred pounds, though Sam's hair was black and Matt's was brown. They knew each other well after riding over thousands of miles and surviving hundreds of fights. An unfortunate result of the many shoot-outs they had survived was that they were developing a reputation as gunfighters.

The two were natural warriors. Sam's father, Medicine Horse, had been killed during the Battle of the Little Big Horn after he charged Custer, alone, unarmed except for a coup stick. Before that battle, realizing the inevitability of war, the chief had ordered Sam from the Indian encampment, to adopt the white man's ways and to forever forget his Cheyenne blood. Though Sam had kept that promise, it often was difficult as he felt himself pulled in the direction of two different cultures.

Matt and Sam had witnessed the subsequent slaughter at the Little Big Horn, though that was a secret only they shared. During the time following the death of Sam's father, Sam and Matt had decided to drift for a time in an effort to erase the terrible memory of the battle. They were often mistaken for out-of-work drifters, but were actually well-educated and wealthy. Sam Two-Wolves had attended an Eastern college, graduating with honors, and Matt had been educated at home by his mother, a school teacher. Sam's mother had come from a rich Eastern family, and Matt had earned his fortune through hard work, riding shotgun for gold shipments and as an army scout and investing his money in land. Matt and Sam now owned profitable cattle and horse ranches along the Wyoming-Montana border.

Ahead of them flowed a clear stream past a stand of trees. Sam shook his head, breathed deeply. "I'm not even going to let you spoil my day!" he said. "It's just good to see grass and trees again. This place looks promising."

"It does look good. And I'm looking forward to some real fishing. It's been a while since I've had a chance to lean back and drown some worms." He stepped out of his saddle and found a gentle swell near the water. "This place is for me. Once I cut a pole, I'll be in good shape."

Sam got off his horse, then started to go through his packs. "You plan to catch anything?" he asked with a straight face.

"Enough to fill our bellies," Matt said.

"Think there's enough fish in that stream for that?"

"Enough for a start."

"Then we need some more supplies. We're out of flour and just about out of salt. There's supposed to be a town a little farther down."

"You go on in and take care of the groceries. I'm going to get a head start on supper." He ran his hand along a sapling. "This looks like it'll do."

"The old ways are still the best."

"You bet." Matt added in a conversational tone, "You're just going in for a few supplies, right? Think maybe you can stay out of trouble this time? I'd hate to interrupt my fishing to rescue you from some mischief!"

"Just save some fish for me." Sam laughed. "I plan to be back by supper."

Chapter 2

It was all Lilly Brandom could do to keep from crying as she rode slowly into town, her son beside her on the wagon. The sun was still shining, the grass was still green, but suddenly the world had changed. She had lost her husband; her son had lost his father. Jack had already been buried, since the thought of his body being torn and mutilated by the coyotes was more than Lilly could stand. There had been no time to grieve, and the full impact of the murder still hadn't hit them. She kept thinking about the fields to be plowed, the seed to be planted, the work to be done. She kept hearing her husband's no-nonsense voice in the house they had built together.

Lilly was working now from sheer guts, keeping her emotions under control until she could report the crime to Marshal Holt. She remembered that Jack used to say something about Holt not being much of a lawman, but with Jack gone she didn't know where else to turn.

As the woman drove the wagon into Snake Creek, she thought again about how the town was almost as ugly as its name. She had never liked the town, even though the acres Jack had bought outside of town were good ones. She compromised by letting her husband do all the errands in town while she stayed on the homestead. Sometimes he would bring back the latest news; but she usually preferred to talk about other subjects, and Jack finally stopped sharing the latest gossip with her. Lilly now wished she had paid a little more attention. She wondered how many friends Jack had in town and how many knew about the man who had murdered her husband.

The town was fairly new, but the buildings—a few stores, saloons, and gaming houses—already looked old and faded. She passed them by, barely seeing them, trying to locate the jail. Lilly jumped as she passed the Black Bull Saloon and a young man stepped out. King Petty tipped his hat mockingly and leered at her. Tommy clenched his fists and started to stand. Lilly placed her hand on his arm, stopping him, as the wagon passed.

Petty laughed.

The jail was at the end of the street. The building was small and looked in even worse shape than the rest of the town. A man lounged in a chair in front of the building. His belly stuck out of an unbuttoned shirt, and his suspenders were almost off his shoulders. Apparently he hadn't shaved in days. Lilly wondered why the marshal didn't run the bum out of town or put him inside the jail where he belonged.

The woman parked the wagon and climbed down. The unkempt man opened his eyes and watched her approach. He said nothing as she brushed past him and entered the jail, her son close behind. The room was a mess, with papers scattered on the floor and the cell doors open.

Lilly went back outside, but nobody was on the street except for the man still sitting in front of the jail.

"Howdy doing, ma'am," he said. "Looking for somebody or something?"

"Do you know where I could find Marshal Holt?"

"Reckon I do. You're looking at him."

Lilly's heart sank. If this was the law in Snake Creek, she knew there'd be little or no chance of bringing her husband's murderer to justice. Even so, her daddy, and then her husband, had stressed the importance of the law and following the law. Now that she was on her own, she had to try.

"My name's Lillian Brandom. My husband, son, and me have been working that valley a few miles outside of town."

"Your husband Jack Brandom? I've seen him around town a few times. Quiet man. Doesn't make much trouble. I like that."

"He's dead."

Holt blinked and scratched his belly. "The hell you say. How'd it happen?"

"He was murdered. And I want you to bring the murderer to justice."

The marshal stood slowly, pulling up his suspenders and looking thoughtful. "Murdered, you say? That's not an easy crime to solve. You need evidence. Eyewitnesses. Investigation takes time. Months. Maybe years."

"I have all the evidence I need. I can identify the murderer."

"Might not even be in my jurisdiction if it happened outside the city limits."

Tommy took a step forward. "We saw my dad's killer when we came through town," he said. "Go arrest him."

"And who do you think that was?" Holt asked.

"Don't know his name. He was down at the Black Bull Saloon."

Holt's face turned white. "Come to think of it, I'm remembering your husband real well," he said. "Got into lots of fights. Couldn't handle his liquor. I'm surprised he didn't get killed before now. He probably got what he deserved."

Lilly threw herself at the marshal, trying to hit him with her fists. "You're a liar!" she cried. "My husband was a good man. What are you trying to do?"

Rough hands suddenly grabbed her, pinning her arms to her side. She struggled but could not get away. Holt had hold of the boy.

"What's happening here, Marshal?"

"Hey, King. This woman claims her husband was murdered."

Lilly looked around her, saw that King Petty was the man who had her in a viselike grip. Several of his men were spaced around them.

"That's the murderer!" Tommy screamed. "That's the man who killed my father!"

"Yeah, I killed the bastard this morning. He was causing trouble."

"Just like I thought," Holt said, wiping his face with a dirty arm, holding on to Tommy with the other. "Jack Brandom was a troublemaker. So it wasn't murder. Looks to me like an open and shut case. Glad you stopped by, King, to straighten out the mess."

Lilly tried to spit at Holt, but King kept her off balance and she missed. Lilly struggled even harder, but King Petty held her so tight that it hurt.

"The woman is upset about the loss of her husband, though from what I've seen it was a small loss," Petty said. "I think, however, there is a law against spreading rumors about law-abiding citizens such as myself. Isn't there, Holt?"

"You're right. There is a law like that. Want me to arrest the woman?"

Tommy struggled, almost got away. Petty gestured to one of his men. "Conn, take that kid and keep him out of my hair for a while. Don't hurt him too bad, unless he gives you trouble. Marshal, you've done your usual fine job; now go on about your business." He dragged the woman toward the Black Bull. "I've got my own business to handle. Me and the widow woman are going to do some talking. We need to reach some kind of understanding before she says anything else bad about me. I think she'll figure it out soon enough."

Sam Two-Wolves whistled softly as he stopped his horse in front of the general store in Snake Creek. He had enjoyed the ride in the sunshine into town, the spring weather warmed his soul, and he was going to have some fresh fried fish for supper. He felt at peace with the world and planned to let nothing interfere with his happiness—not even this shabby little town. All he needed was a few supplies. He'd quickly take care of his business and be back in camp in a matter of hours. Matt was a fair fisherman, but Sam knew a few tricks that his father had taught him that should let him even up the catch in spite of Matt's head start. It was a friendly rivalry, and Sam chuckled at the contest in which both blood brothers would be the winners when it came time to cooking the catch that night.

The town itself was better than some he had seen in his travels, worse than others. With a practiced eye he noted the arrangement of buildings on the short main street, the alleys, the places where a man might hide if he wanted to ambush another. Few people were out, and most of them seemed to be drifters or unsavory types who didn't bother to hide their hostility as they watched him pass. Sam pretended to pay them no mind but made sure his gun was within easy reach, if necessary.

The general store was located a few buildings down from the jail, surrounded by saloons. As Sam tied his horse to a rail in front of the general store, he noticed a slim, attractive woman and a boy walk around a dishevelled man to enter the jail. He smiled at the warm sight of a mother and son and entered the store to take care of his business.

An older man and woman were behind the counter, stacking cans of peaches. Sam decided to take a few of those, as well. It'd be a good dessert following the fish that night.

"Howdy, ma'am," he said. "I'm looking for some supplies."

"You're new in town. You one of King Petty's men?"

"Shush," the man said nervously. "Let's not look for trouble."

"Oh, you hush," she answered.

"I'm nobody's man but my own," Sam replied.

"Good answer. What do you need?"

Sam walked toward the counter, taking a closer look at the woman. She had high cheekbones and dark skin, as if she also had Indian blood in her. Her eyes were dark, but with a slight twinkle. He couldn't tell how old she was, though there was gray in her hair. He handed her the list of supplies.

"We can help you," she said. "I didn't mean to be rude. My name's Clarissa Ponder. This is my husband, Henry."

"Throw in some of those peaches," Sam said. "And who is King Petty?"

"Thinks he owns the town," Clarissa said.

"He does," her husband added. "He's a helluva mean sonofabitch. Fast with a gun. Dangerous. He and his men do pretty much what they want, when they want. They come in here and take without paying for it. It's kind of a sore point with my wife."

"I wouldn't think you'd be too pleased, either," Sam said.

"Damned right I'm not, but I don't see that we have much choice in the matter. If it's a question of losing a few dollars in goods or losing your life, I'll choose living every time."

Sam acted as if he were looking at a barrel of coffee, but was actually watching the man's face. There was anger and hurt in his eyes. It bothered him to have to give in to Petty and his men, but he was obviously not a gunfighter. He was an older man trying to run a business in a struggling town. He wouldn't have a chance against Petty. Henry Ponder was just doing the best he could.

"Come to think of it, I could use some of this coffee, as well," Sam said.

Clarissa came out from behind the counter. Her eyes looked over Sam, stopped at the necklace around his throat, made up of multicolored stones pierced by rawhide. Matt wore an identical necklace. She glanced into Sam's face, started to say something, then changed her mind as she returned to the other side of the counter.

"You just passing through?" Henry asked. He wrapped the items while Clarissa totalled the bill.

"Planning to do a little fishing," Sam answered.

"Good pastime. Always figured a man couldn't get in too much trouble with a fishing pole in his hand."

Loud voices started to drift through the open door. Henry looked nervously toward the street. Clarissa said angrily, "You wanted to know about King Petty. I'd lay odds that he's out there, causing trouble again."

Sam stepped casually to the door and looked toward the jail in time to see a young man grab hold of a woman and start to drag her down the street. Another man held the boy.

"Who are they?" Sam asked.

"The woman is Lilly Brandom," Clarissa said. "The boy is her son. It's odd to see her in town. Usually her husband comes in by himself to buy supplies."

"And the man holding her?"

"King Petty himself."

Sam sighed. He knew better than to get involved,

but he couldn't walk away and let a woman and her son be treated that way. He placed some cash on the counter and said, "I may be in town for a while, after all. Go ahead and start an account for me." He checked the action of his Colt and said, "I'll be back in a few minutes to pick up my stuff."

"I told you that Petty is dangerous and mean," Henry said. "He's killed lots of men. I'd think twice before I go out there."

Sam shrugged.

Clarissa added, "We never did catch your name to put on your bill."

"Sam Two-Wolves."

Henry looked surprised and Clarissa smiled. Henry exclaimed, "The gunfighter?"

"No . . . just a fisherman. If I'm lucky."

It was nothing unusual to see King Petty throwing his weight around town, though it still generated a certain amount of attention. Faces had gathered at doors and windows up and down the street to watch the scene in front of the jail. On the street itself were Petty's men. Everybody, law-abiding citizens and criminals, all knew the plans that Petty had for Lilly, but nobody lifted a hand to help her.

Petty knew they wouldn't.

"Come along, woman, spend a little time with a real man and you'll forget that dead husband of yours. Hell, you'll probably even thank me!"

The woman still struggled, even though Petty gripped her arm so tightly that she knew escape was impossible. Behind him, Petty could hear the kid yelling, trying not to cry. It was a nuisance and a distraction that he would deal with later. For now, he had the woman.

Petty stopped as a tall, dark-haired man stood in front of him.

"Move. Out of my way."

"I'd like to talk with the woman."

"Nope. She's mine."

Petty was surprised that the other man not only didn't move, but he spoke directly to Lilly. "Am I to assume that this gentleman's attentions are uninvited and unwanted?" he asked.

"I want nothing to do with him, except to see him dead."

"The name's Sam Two-Wolves, and I'll see what I can do." He turned to Petty and said conversationally, "Let her go."

The street was suddenly quiet. Sam stood his ground, apparently unconcerned that he was outnumbered and that Petty was supposed to be the most dangerous man in the area. Petty looked Sam over as he motioned some of his men forward.

"You're not even worth the trouble it'd take to kill you," Petty said. "Giles, Hamm, take care of this for me, would you?"

Giles was the first to draw, but was dead before the gun could clear leather. Sam had pulled his own Colt with blinding speed and sent a slug of death toward the outlaw. The bullet hit Giles cleanly in the chest, throwing him backward into the dusty street.

Sam pivoted, and fell to the ground as Hamm managed to squeeze off two shots, both missing their target by a wide margin. Sam rolled, came up in a crouch, took aim and fired another shot. This one hit Hamm in the neck. The outlaw dropped his gun, staggered three steps, and then fell lifeless near the other dead man.

Petty remained cool. This was something new, for somebody to be almost as good with a gun as he was. Sam had drawn and fired with a casual grace and with unerring accuracy. Petty knew this man could be trouble. He loosened his grip, and the woman pulled away, running toward her son.

Sam stood and said, "Let the boy go, as well."

Conn did so. Tommy ran and wrapped his arms around his mother.

"Any other discussion?" Sam said.

Petty smiled. "Not right now. But we'll meet again. You can count on it."

"I'll look forward to it."

Petty started for the Black Bull. He said to his men without looking back, "Get rid of that trash on the street. I'm going for a drink. All this excitement's made me thirsty."

Sam gently guided the woman and child out of the street toward Ponder's store.

Chapter 3

Matt Bodine took his time as he selected the sapling to use as his fishing pole, attached the line and hook, then walked along the creek bank with a can of worms, looking for just the right spot. He knew how to use the fancy gear that the Easterners seemed to prefer, and he could patiently stalk fish with spear and net as the Indians did. Sometimes, however, he preferred a simple pole on a creek bank and let nature take its course. It was less work and a lot more relaxing.

He finally found what he was looking for: a gentle hill, covered with short grass, with a tall tree to provide shade. In the creek itself was enough brush to provide shelter for the fish, but not so much as to tangle the line. Matt expected no trouble, but still made a quick search of the area before he sat down on the bank. He had learned a long time ago a person couldn't be too careful, that trouble often came when least expected. All he found this time was cattle sign.

Matt leaned back, dipped the hook in the water, and waited. The first nibble came within minutes. Matt watched the line patiently, set the hook at just the right

instant and yanked the fish from the water, chuckling
softly to himself. Matt knew that Sam considered himself an expert fisherman, and that when he got back
there would be a friendly competition about who
caught the most fish for supper. Maybe it wasn't fair
for Matt to get a head start, but it would be funny to
see Sam's face when he saw he was beat before he even
started! Matt would make things even by cooking supper that night without complaint. If his luck continued, he'd have plenty of time to get the meal cooked
before Sam returned.

After an hour, the nibbles slowed, but not enough
for Matt to move on. He was putting another worm on
a hook when he heard sounds around him from two
different directions. He instantly crouched down and
pulled his Colt revolver from its holster. One sound
was soft as the grass swayed. Matt knew it was a snake
of some kind and turned his attention to the louder
sound of something crashing through the underbrush.

A large bull stuck its head through the bushes and
glared at Matt with red eyes.

Matt laughed. He had been around cattle all his life,
owned a ranch in Wyoming, and could cowboy with
the best of them. A bull, even a mean one, didn't
bother him. If it waded into the creek, however, it
would disturb the water and probably ruin fishing for
the rest of the day.

"Go on, old boy," Matt said, putting his gun back
in its holster. "Just move your hide and get your drink
elsewhere." The bull snorted. It was a solid-looking
animal that appeared as if it could be the sire of a good
herd. Matt could appreciate such an animal, but he
didn't want the blamed thing looking over his shoul-

der as he fished. Matt moved a step closer, ready to slap the animal in the face to get it started. "I said get out of here."

The bull snorted again and took a step away from Matt, putting its foot down on the tail of a snake that was slithering through the grass. The snake, startled, bit the bull on its hind leg. It turned its red eyes on Matt, as if it blamed the man for the pain, and attacked.

Matt jumped and sidestepped. He could feel the animal's large horns whistle past his head. The bull kicked as it raced past, overturning Matt's bucket of worms and the fish he had caught, then turned to face him again. Matt glanced at the empty bucket. The results of the afternoon's effort were gone. It aggravated Matt, who was tempted to shoot the critter on general principle, but he hated to waste such a fine-looking animal if it could be helped. Matt generally worked with cattle from the back of a horse, not on foot, and he didn't particularly like being at the disadvantage.

The bull charged again. Matt waited until the last minute, then ducked beneath the sharp horns and grabbed the animal by the neck, trying to wrestle it to the ground. Most men would have been thrown within seconds, but Matt held tightly, his muscles bulging with the effort. He finally got the leverage he needed, and the bull started to fall slowly to the ground. Matt released his grip and jumped out of the way as the animal finally hit the dirt.

Matt took off his hat to slap the critter's behind and send it along its way. He wanted only to go back to his fishing—if there were still any fish that weren't scared away—when an angry voice called out, "I got you in my sights. You've rustled the last of our cattle, and I don't care what your boss says. You got our cows. I seen your tracks. But damned if you're going to take my bull."

Ralph Smiley was having a good time. He had been in the cattle rustling business for a long time, but the job had never been as easy as it had been since joining up with King Petty's outfit. In the old days, Smiley always had to watch his back trail, since some irate rancher or lawman seemed to be after him, just because he took their critters. It made for some close calls.

Smiley still followed his old habits, working mainly at night, away from the main herds, trying to cover his tracks, even though there really wasn't any need. With Petty, it was almost like a regular job. Petty had everybody so boogered that they left him—and anybody associated with him—alone. So it was a simple matter for Smiley and his men to go into a range, round up the choice animals, and herd them into the hidden valley until the rustlers had gathered enough to drive the cattle to market.

Smiley rode leisurely, almost absentmindedly keeping the stolen animals on track. This bunch came from range used by Lester Brown and his son. Those two always made a lot of noise, but they were both as intimidated as everybody else. They might threaten, but they were no real danger.

Or were they?

Smiley paused and scratched his black beard as a

figure rode toward him. The other hands looked to him for directions. He motioned for them to keep on with their work but to keep a close watch. They continued with the cattle when the rider got close enough for Smiley to recognize old man Brown. The exception was Ash Crawford, whose job was not to look after the cattle but to ensure that Smiley did his job. He looked busy, but rode close enough to hear Smiley's talk with Brown.

The outlaw loosened the Colt in his holster and leaned back in the saddle, waiting for the visitor. Brown was, as expected, hopping mad. His eyes seemed to shoot fire through bushy gray eyebrows, and his mouth was set in a firm frown. Some said he had been fairly good with a gun when he was younger, but since the death of his young wife had kept to himself. Smiley figured Brown was too old now to cause serious trouble.

"Those are my cattle," Brown said as soon as he was within shouting distance.

"They *were* your cattle," Smiley corrected. The end of the small herd was now passing. "Now they're mine. And King Petty's."

"Do you have to stand behind that punk kid to protect you? Throwing his name around doesn't mean a thing to me."

"Maybe these were your animals," Smiley said. He was enjoying himself. It wasn't often in his life that he clearly had the upper hand. "But there's been a change in ownership. And as for Petty, last dozen men tried to fight him are pushing daisies. I'd think twice before you do anything stupid."

Brown, even in his anger, recognized that he had no

resources in this fight. Ash and two of Smiley's men were already coming over to join in the talk. Brown knew he was outnumbered and would be killed if he even acted like he would reach for his gun.

"So you win again," Brown finally said, slowly. "I'll leave peaceably, though it pains me no end to see the herd I've worked toward for years just walking away from me."

"Yeah. Such a sad sight. Is that why you came all the way out here—to kiss your ranch goodbye?"

"I planned to shoot you, no matter the trouble it might cause me with your boss. Even if it meant my getting killed. I wasn't going to put up with your crap anymore."

"You gave up that idea?"

"Nothing I can do here. I know you think Petty rules this country, but I'm warning you that will change. I swear that I'll find some way to get my cattle back. And I plan to see you dead, one way or another."

"Not a chance, old man. I don't take kindly to threats, but I'll overlook it because of your age. If you turn that horse around and get out of here, I'll let you live a little while longer."

"You're a real bastard, Smiley."

"Right. Petty likes that in a man. Now get out of here. If I see you again, I may have to shoot you."

Smiley turned his attention back to the cattle as Brown rode away. The outlaw figured he had seen the last of Brown.

*   *   *

Matt shook his head slowly to clear it. He didn't want to admit it to himself, but the fight with the bull had left him temporarily drained. He turned toward the direction from where the voice had come.

"We have some kind of misunderstanding," Matt said, standing to his full height. "I'm not after your cattle."

"No talk. Just stand still. When Pa gets back, we'll figure what to do with you."

Matt breathed slowly, clearing his head. He stretched aching muscles, relaxing his gun arm, loosening his fingers. He had to play for time. The man who had gotten the drop on him hadn't wanted to kill him very badly, else he would have shot already.

"Why don't you come out and let me see you?" Matt said. "I'm obviously no danger as long as your gun is on me."

A tall man stepped out from behind some brush. He was blond-headed, as tall as Matt but not as muscular, and held a rifle aimed at Matt's belly.

"Don't try any funny stuff," he said.

"Not me," Matt said. "I would never tell a joke to a hostile audience."

The other man looked at him with a puzzled expression.

"If I were you, I wouldn't be telling jokes in a situation like this."

"Who's joking? I'm just making conversation. Being friendly. What's your name, friend? And why the big iron?"

"You're an odd one. Not like the others. I'm Derrell Brown, and the reason for the gun is that I don't like rustlers."

"I'll say it again, friend, this is obviously a case of mistaken identity. My name is Matthew Bodine and I'm not a cattle rustler. Even if I was, I wouldn't try to steal a bull by riding him away! I'm just here to do a little fishing."

"Just interested in fishing? The way you're wearing that six-gun on your hip?"

"A man never knows when he'll be threatened by somebody holding a rifle on him."

"You have an answer for everything?"

"Don't believe I've been fishing instead of rustling? I can prove it. I left my pole by the creek. Take a look."

Derrell glanced toward the creek just for an instant, but it was long enough for Matt to make his move. The other man was big, strong, and probably competent. But he apparently lacked the experience and expertise that Matt had accumulated over many years and countless miles of adventures. Matt leaped and hit the ground in a roll, safely underneath the path of any rifle bullet.

Surprisingly, Derrell didn't shoot. He did bring the barrel down, trying to use it as a club against Matt, but missed as Matt continued to roll. He came up just inches from where Derrell was standing and drove his shoulder into the other man's belly.

Derrell staggered, but didn't fall. He dropped the rifle, brought both fists together and hit Matt on the back of his neck.

The blow almost stunned Matt. Normally, he would have shrugged off such a punch, but he was still tired. Derrell raised his fists to try again. Just as his hands came down, Matt purposely fell to the ground. Derrell was thrown offbalance, toppling forward. Matt spun around the other man and stood, lashing out with a solid kick to Derrell's behind, sending him sprawling to the ground.

Matt pounced on his opponent, delivering a solid blow to Derrell's face. Derrell took the blows without flinching, then with a mighty heave sent Matt sailing over him. A trickle of blood was dripping from Derrell's nose, but it didn't slow him down. He moved in on Matt with a combination of rights and lefts that Matt had difficulty blocking, pushing him back toward the water's edge.

Matt had to admit that the other man was a good fighter. He had a lot of heart and good instincts, but in his inexperience he made too many errors. All Matt had to do was to be patient and wait for the other man to make a mistake.

Matt finally found the opening he had been looking for at the water's edge. Derrell dropped his guard for an instant. Matt's hand whipped out and landed with a loud whump in Derrell's belly. The blow knocked the breath out of him, which gave Matt the chance to rapidly deliver more blows to the stomach and head.

Derrell struck out with a wild punch that glanced off Matt's shoulder. It had little force, but threw Matt off balance. Derrell got him in a bear hug, threw him into the water, then jumped in after him.

Matt's fist was just rising out of the water when the gunshot exploded from the creek bank and the bullet hit the ground a few feet in front of Derrell and Matt.

The bullet had broken the back of the snake that was now writhing closer and closer to the water.

Another shot was fired. This one neatly separated the snake's head from its body, sending it flying through the air and landing in the water near Matt's face.

Chapter 4

Sam gently guided the woman and boy down the street toward Ponder's store. A small crowd remained behind, watching the bodies being carried away. Sam appeared indifferent, but was ready for trouble. Petty and his men entered one of the saloons. Sam knew he had made an enemy, but he didn't care. He had done what was right, and that was the important thing.

The woman tried to act strong, but her walk was slightly unsteady, as if she had been drinking. Sam knew that though he had saved her from Petty's intentions, something terrible had already happened.

Henry Ponder was near the door when Sam reached the store with the woman and boy. He was holding a shotgun. His hands nervously moved up and down the barrel, but he didn't stop them from entering. Clarissa was at a stove in the corner, boiling water for tea.

"Sam Two-Wolves, in my store," Ponder said. "I've heard stories about how fast you and your partner, Matt Bodine, are with your guns. I figured they were exaggerated. I was wrong. You sure made short work of Petty's men out there."

"Petty didn't draw on me," Sam noted.

"He's mean and sneaky. He'll bide his time until he's good and ready. He'll try to surprise you or shoot you in the back."

"Won't be the first man to try that, and probably won't be the last," Sam answered.

He directed the woman toward a chair near the stove. Clarissa took over from there, talking to her softly as she prepared the tea. Sam walked silently across the floor and pulled up another chair to face the woman. She looked up at him with big eyes, and said sincerely, "Thank you."

"You're welcome. Now that I'm involved, you want to tell me your story? What have you got to do with King Petty?"

The woman shuddered. Clarissa handed a cup of tea to Sam and asked, "Would you give this to Lilly?"

As Sam took the cup, he noted some other scents besides tea in the cup. Apparently Clarissa had added some herbs to calm and heal, much as Sam's mother had done when he was a child. Sam passed the cup to Lillian.

"My name's Lilly Brandom. This is my son, Tommy. Up until this morning, we had nothing to do with Petty. I just barely knew the name. I hardly ever come to town, letting my husband do whatever business needed doing."

"So what happened this morning?" Sam questioned.

"Petty rode up to our homestead and shot my husband—just for the hell of it. And because he said he wanted me."

Clarissa gasped at the news. Henry shook his head sadly and asked, "He killed Jack?"

"We buried him this morning. Me and my son."

Sam knew there was nothing he could say that would help lessen the loss. So he said simply, "I'm sorry."

"He was a quiet man," Henry said. "He was a good man, I think. Never got into trouble. To my knowledge, he never even took a drink. He did business with Clarissa and me. We gave him credit, and he always found some way to pay us back."

"Did he do . . . anything to you?" Clarissa asked.

"No. He threatened to come back later. When he felt like it."

"Then what are you doing in town, girl? If he's after you, that's asking for trouble!"

"I thought maybe . . . the marshal could do something."

Henry laughed without humor. "Holt? He's about as incompetent as they come. He follows Petty's orders."

"I had to do something," Lilly said, her lower lip quivering. "I couldn't just sit around and wait for that . . . monster . . . to come back. I didn't know what else to do."

Clarissa patted the woman on the shoulder. "That's all right," Clarissa said. "That's all right."

Tommy was standing near his mother. He had been silent from the time of the shoot-out in the street. He finally spoke up, looking directly at Sam. "You weren't afraid," Tommy said. "Everybody else is afraid of Petty. But you're not afraid. Could you help us? Could you kill the man that murdered my daddy?"

Sam sensed some of the fire that was burning in the boy. The loss was still too new; he was still in a state of shock. The true anger and hurt would come later. Sam did not want to give a flippant answer, but he also had to be truthful.

"I don't work that way," Sam said. "I don't kill in cold blood, not even rabid dogs like Petty."

"But if you don't do it, nobody will!" Tommy said.

Sam felt uncomfortable, but he was the one who had placed himself in the situation.

"Tell you what. I plan to be in the area for a few days. Maybe I can be of some help. I can at least talk to the marshal for you. I'm making no promises. So don't get your hopes up."

"Thank you, Mr. Two-Wolves."

"Call me Sam." He turned to Ponder. "Henry, how about my supplies?"

At the counter, the store owner asked softly, "Don't underestimate Petty. He'll be gunning for you."

"That's one reason I'll be sticking around for a while. I'd rather keep an eye on him than have him surprise me down the road."

"You seriously thinking about trying to help Lilly?"

"You and I both know she needs more than the kind of help I could give. She needs friends to see her through this time. She needs somebody to help her work her homestead. She needs time. I might help hand out a little justice, but it won't bring her husband back."

"You're good, Sam. Maybe the best. But you don't know King Petty. You need somebody to watch your back. Where is your partner, anyway?"

"Matt is out where I should be. Fishing. And staying out of trouble. I hope."

Not much scared Matt Bodine, and certainly not snakes. But there was something unsettling about seeing a snake's head land just inches from his face. Matt instinctively jumped backward to get away from the snake. Derrell Brown did the same in the opposite direction. The movement made the water ripple and the snake's head dance up and down.

Matt and Brown watched the snake's head in awkward silence, which was suddenly punctuated by a deep belly laugh.

"You two were so busy fighting each other you almost got your asses bit," the voice said as it laughed. "Lucky for you I came back when I did."

"That wasn't funny, Pa," Derrell said.

An older man stepped into the clearing near the creek, still laughing. He held a rifle in his hands.

"Oh, I don't know. You should have seen your faces when that snake's head landed between you two! It was tolerably fair shooting for an old man, if I do say so myself."

Matt's eyes were hard for long seconds, then softened as he also started to laugh. Soon, Derrell had joined in.

"Yes, it was decent shooting," Matt agreed.

"If you two are through fighting, come on out of the water and let's talk." He pointed his gun at Matt. "Don't forget, I have the gun pointed at your belly. If you were thinking of trying anything, that is."

Matt raised his hands in a gesture of peace.

"All I want to do is a little fishing," he said, following Derrell out of the water.

"Then what's the fighting all about?"

"I was just minding my own business when one of your damned bulls tried to run me off. I don't run off too easy, and convinced the old boy to leave me alone. Next thing I know your son is after me. Are you just naturally unfriendly, or what?"

"I thought he was one of the rustlers, Pa," Derrell explained.

"Rustler problems?" Matt said. "That I can understand. My camp's a little ways down the creek. Let's get a fire going, boil some coffee, and see if we can't start over again."

The older man held out his hand. "My name's Lester Brown. This is my son, Derrell. Some fresh coffee sounds mighty good."

"I'm Matt Bodine. Come along and I'll get you that coffee."

Matt led the way, shaking his head in frustration at the bank where he had been fishing, now churned into a muddy mess. The fish he had caught for supper had been lost. Well, it couldn't be helped now. There was still time to catch some more fish.

Matt walked to the water's edge and picked up his pole.

"This is a good spot," Brown said. "Or was a good spot. Fish are probably all scared away now. But there's a better place a little downstream and around the bend. After that coffee, I'll be glad to show you. It's the least I could do after the way my son treated you."

"On the other hand, you did save us both from being snake-bit."

"Water moccasins," Brown said. "This part of the country is full of them. Sometimes it seems you can't even walk more than a few feet without stepping on a dozen of them. I've been here for years and still can't get used to it. That's how the town got its name, you know. Snake Creek. That's what this place is called, too. Confusing? Not if you've been here awhile."

Matt was used to making accurate judgments about people. Though he was still irritated at Derrell's attack on him, Matt found himself liking Brown and his son. Derrell had put up a good fight, and rustler problems did tend to make a person a little quick on the draw. When they reached the camp, Matt finished the coffee, filled the cups, and sat back on the ground near the fire.

"Now tell me about your rustling problem," Matt urged.

Brown sighed and pushed his tattered hat back on his head. "I've been ranching in this part of the country for almost twenty years," he said. "Most of that time was on my own. It was tough, lonely work, but I made a go of it. Then I found Mollie, bless her soul, and we had Derrell. It's just been him and me for a long time, but we've added to the herd. I've faced winter storms, droughts, and too many men who tried to take away from me what I've built and hoped to pass on to my son. Nothing's gotten the better of me until King Petty came along."

"Another rancher?" Matt asked. "An outlaw?"

"One helluva mean sonofabitch," Brown said, his gray eyebrows arching together. "He'd just as soon kill you as talk with you. He's got the whole town afraid of its own shadow. Everybody's scared of him. Other riffraff know a good thing when they see it, so joined up with him. Ralph Smiley's one of them."

Matt said thoughtfully, "I've heard of him. A small-time crook. Never amounted to much."

"He's hooked up with Petty and has been stealing this area blind. He finally got to my spread last night. I tracked them for a few miles and like a fool confronted him. Almost got myself killed. But doing nothing leaves a bad taste in my mouth. I haven't worked this hard for this long just to give it up now."

"Any plans?"

"Still working on them. I know I'm not going to just roll over and play dead."

"Don't blame you. I wish you luck. Now how about showing me that good fishing spot . . ."

King Petty stared moodily at the ceiling of the Black Bull Saloon, which he owned. He had taken it from the original owner years ago and now used it as his private club. The girls that were usually on his lap were keeping their distance, as were his men. He had an open bottle of whiskey on the table in front of him.

Petty's thoughts kept returning to the Brandom woman and how easily the stranger, Sam Two-Wolves, had taken her from him. His draw was almost as fast as Petty's, and he didn't back away from a fight as did everybody else in town. Two-Wolves could be a problem.

On the other hand, Petty was bored with the way things had been. Two-Wolves might present a challenge to him, to make life a little more interesting before he was killed. After all, Petty could also make life interesting for Two-Wolves.

Petty was not about to let Two-Wolves get away with humiliating him and killing his men.

He gulped his drink, poured another, and thought again about Lilly Brandom. She was a desirable woman. He had wanted her before. Now he had to have her. Two-Wolves had seen to that. Nobody told King Petty what to do, when to do it, or who to do it with.

He slammed the glass on the table and yelled, "Conn! Get over here!"

The tall man at the bar strolled over to Petty's table.

"Find Holt."

"Sure, boss. But what do you want with that clown?"

"I want to talk to him. He ain't worth much, but he is the marshal. We might be able to use that as a weapon against Two-Wolves. Maybe we can find some way to make his stay in town a little more uncomfortable."

"Don't think Two-Wolves is going to scare easy."

"Or, if we can't get to him, then maybe the widow Brandom. We'll come up with something. One way or another, I plan to have the widow. And I plan to kill Sam Two-Wolves."

Chapter 5

Lilly had been quiet ever since they had left Ponder's store. Sam, holding the reins of the woman's wagon, knew that the reason for her calm was partly due to the mixture that Clarissa had prepared for her. It wasn't a drug, but a combination of herbs known to some Indians and old-timers used to temporarily soothe nervous problems. It would also help her to sleep when she returned home. Unfortunately, it would not make the following days any easier to accept.

Sam could tell a lot about a man by the way he treated his animals, and he respected the late Jack Brandom. The two horses pulling the wagon were not fancy, but they were sturdy and healthy. They had been worked, but they had also been well-fed and groomed. Sam figured Jack Brandom would have been a no-nonsense kind of man, a hard worker, somebody who probably tried to take care of his family the best way he knew how.

Sam watched Lilly as they rode. She was a very attractive woman, with soft hair and curves in all the right places. She seemed to be in her twenties, which would mean that she had married young. That would not be unusual. Even in her grief, she was protective of her son, and the sorrow at the loss of her husband seemed genuine.

Sam sympathized with Lilly and Tommy. Though in town he had tried to discourage any idea of his taking revenge on King Petty, Sam knew he could not walk away from this fight. This killing was so cruel and senseless that Sam knew he had to do something, though he wasn't sure what that would be. For now, his action was only to try to see the mother and son safely home. He had placed the supplies purchased from the Ponders in bags on his horse, tied behind the wagon.

This part of the country consisted of gently rolling hills covered with grass and trees, leading to deeper valleys near the town. The wagon moved slowly. Lilly's body swayed gracefully on the seat.

"Lilly, I said back in town that I might try to help you. To do that, I need more information. Do you feel up to it?" The woman nodded her head. "Tell me exactly what happened."

"It all happened so fast, it's almost like a blur," Lilly said. "One minute, Jack's in the field, breaking ground for planting. Tommy's helping him. I bring them some water and Tommy comes with me back to the house. Next thing I know, I hear two shots and I see that . . . Petty riding over the hill and bragging that he shot my husband."

"Did Jack have any enemies? Could he have some-how provoked the fight?"

"I don't think so . . . I know he didn't. Petty bragged

that he killed Jack in cold blood. He . . . killed him . . ."

Suddenly, Lilly started crying. Sam stopped the wagon, touched the woman on the shoulder, and she fell into his arms, sobs rocking her body. The boy didn't cry, but he moved closer to her. Sam put his arms around both of them, wishing he could do more.

Richard Holt had no illusions that he had been appointed City Marshal only because he was so worthless. Petty had killed the previous three men who had held the position, and the "city fathers" had all but given up on appointing another. Holt was handpicked by Petty as a joke. It was a way to thumb his nose at what might have remained of the law in Snake Creek. Holt could handle that, since it meant thirty dollars per month plus room and board for basically sitting around the jail and doing occasional errands for Petty. Even so, he hated to be summoned by Petty, especially after already having such a rough day. Some of the bullets fired by the stranger, Two-Wolves, had come too close to him for comfort. His agreement to serve as marshal hadn't included any actual bullets being shot at him.

Outside the Black Bull Saloon, Holt sighed and tucked in his shirt. Conn, holding the door open in front of him, said, "Come on, King's waiting."

"I'm coming . . . I'm coming."

Petty was seated at a table in the center of the room, an open whiskey bottle in front of him. Several of his men were with him around the table.

"About time, Holt," Petty said. "Next time, don't keep me waiting. Understand?"

"Sure, boss."

"We're discussing ideas about how to have a little fun with the widow Brandom and that troublemaker, Two-Wolves. Any ideas?"

"I don't know . . . you're the boss."

"Damned right. While we were waiting for you, we already came up with a couple of ideas."

"I'm sure they're good ones," Holt said. "I'll be there, whatever you need."

"Good. That's what I want to hear, since you're going to be paying the widow a visit. I want you to worry her a little."

"What do you mean? She might shoot me!" Holt gulped. "Or, worse, Two-Wolves might shoot me."

Petty continued as if he hadn't heard Holt's words. "The woman seems to think that you could actually do something about her husband's death." He laughed. "So let her continue to think that. Ride on out to her place and tell her that you'd be glad to investigate . . . if you have the evidence. So you'll need proof of the killing . . . her husband's body!" Petty laughed even harder. "That should give her some pleasant dreams!"

"Sounds kind of rough on the woman and kid," Holt started to say, then saw the frown on Petty's face. He continued, "What if she tries to shoot me? I didn't make any points with her this afternoon."

"I'll send Conn with you. And don't worry about Two-Wolves." He turned to two of his other men. "Hardesty, Cooper, you two take care of that meddling sonofabitch. He was riding out of town a few

minutes ago with the widow. If you ride fast, you can
probably catch up to him before he gets the woman
home. Ambush him. Catch him by surprise and kill
him quick and you shouldn't have any problem. He
just got lucky this afternoon."

"How about a drink . . . for the road?" Holt asked.

"Later. Now get. You all know what to do. Now do
it."

Matt was almost ready to forget the fishing and just
pull out some bacon and beans for supper. It was now
a matter of honor, however, to have that fish ready
upon Sam's return. And there was still enough day left
to accomplish the task.

After Lester and Derrell Brown had left, Matt
grabbed his pole, found some fresh worms, and tried
the spot that the Browns had recommended. It almost
seemed too shady to Matt's eyes, but the fish were
biting.

Unfortunately, the quiet time he had anticipated
eluded him. The spot was peaceful enough, and the
fishing was relaxing, but he kept thinking about the
rustlers plaguing the Browns, in general, and King
Petty, in particular. Matt had not offered to help them
because it wasn't his fight. He was also still upset at
Derrell's attack on him, even though it was an honest
mistake. Still, Matt hated to turn his back on a fellow
rancher. Matt had also previously worked as a law
officer, and there was something about King Petty that
caused his neck hairs to tingle in warning. It was a
vague feeling, but over the years Matt had learned to
trust his instincts. He felt like he should be doing

something other than holding a fishing rod, even though he was no longer a lawman nor was it his problem.

By mid-afternoon, Matt had caught plenty of fish for supper. Thoughts of the rustlers kept crossing his mind. Almost in spite of himself, and against his better judgment, he pulled his pole out of the water and saddled his horse. He told himself he wasn't going to look for anything in particular; he just wanted to see what he could find.

The Browns had good land, Matt decided as he rode. The grass was thick and there was plenty of water. The signs indicated that they had a fairly large herd.

Matt came upon the trail of the rustlers near a large watering hole about a mile from where he had been fishing. Tracks showed that many cattle had gathered here, but had been herded together by a few men. Matt counted about five different horses, though there could have been more.

The workers were also sloppy in their roundup, missing a few dozen of the animals, which were once again gathered at the water. Matt decided that this meant the rustlers were so sure of themselves that they were not concerned about rounding up all the cattle at one time, that they would be coming back when they were good and ready.

Sam could have read more details in the tracks, but Matt did well enough. He followed the trail for a while, even to the point where Lester Brown had ridden into the moving herd, his horse's tracks mingling with the cattle in the trampled dirt. The trail then led into some rocky ground, but Matt had learned what he needed to know. The rustlers consisted only of a small group, and they weren't too concerned about being followed. If he chose to, Matt could track them to where they were holding the stolen cattle.

His questions answered, Matt turned his horse around to return to his camp. It was time to start cleaning the fish. Sam would probably be back soon, and he might as well be ready.

Just outside of camp, Matt detected a subtle movement in the brush. This time, a flash of sunlight off a gun barrel showed that it was not a snake or a bull. Matt's hand dropped to the revolver at his side. He had it pulled and ready to fire when Lester Brown stepped into the open.

"Hold on, son!" he cried out, holding his rifle in front of him. "Don't shoot!"

"Good way to get yourself killed," Matt said. "You came damned close."

"Hell, I didn't expect you to be so fast. Damned, you had that gun out of its holster before I could even blink. That's about as fast as I've ever seen!"

"So what are you doing out here?"

"I wanted to catch you before you got to your camp. Derrell and I brought you a little gift—some fish that we caught for you—to kind of make up for what you lost earlier. I wanted to warn you that Derrell and me are here, so you wouldn't come in shooting. Looks like a good thing I did!"

"That sounds reasonable," Matt agreed.

"And, with your permission, we'd like to cook supper tonight. It's the least we could do, seeing as to how Derrell tried to take your head off earlier."

"Are you good cooks?" Matt asked, smiling.

"I was a bachelor for most of my life," Brown said. "I learned to be a pretty hot-damned good cook, if I do say so myself. And I taught Derrell everything I know."

"My partner, Sam, is coming in later with some supplies."

"Don't worry about it. We've got plenty of everything."

"Somehow I don't think Sam would object, as long as he doesn't have to cook. Make yourself at home."

Lilly had stopped crying and had moved to the outside edge of the wagon seat. Sam kept his eyes on the road ahead. The way was clear, but he didn't trust Petty at all. It would be just like him to try an ambush of some sort, and there was no use taking chances.

"Will you be staying with us?" Tommy asked.

"Afraid not," Sam answered. "I need to check on my partner, Matt. He and I are camped a little ways downstream."

"Can't Matt get along without you?"

Sam smiled. "I figure Matt can take care of himself. It's more a matter of decorum . . ."

Tommy looked puzzled. "De-corum?" he asked.

"It wouldn't look right for a strange man to be staying with you all so soon after your daddy's death."

Tommy looked disappointed.

"But I'll see you the rest of the way home. And I'll stop by first thing tomorrow."

"Is your partner anything like you?" Lilly asked, with what was almost a smile. Sam figured Clarissa's tea must be working pretty well. "If so, you must make an interesting pair."

"Matt's supposed to be fishing and staying out of trouble," Sam said. "He's a fair fisherman, but he's not any good at all at staying out of trouble."

Lilly looked at him with big, sad eyes.

"Of course, I'm not too good in that department myself," Sam concluded softly, so Lilly wouldn't hear.

The next mile was spent in a pleasant silence, which was interrupted suddenly by a rifle shot from a hill near the Brandom place. Sam immediately pulled Lilly and Tommy to the floor of the wagon. Another shot was fired, hitting the seat just inches from Sam's head.

"I suspect they may be after me," Sam said, returning the fire. "I seem to have that effect on some people."

More shots were fired from the hill and from the other side of the road. It was a classic ambush, but the bushwhackers had gotten careless and made their move too soon. Sam spotted the flashes from the gunshots and spaced his shots carefully. He knew he hadn't hit anything, but he figured he'd probably get the bullets close enough to make his attackers nervous.

The air was suddenly quiet, only to be broken again by the sound of hoofbeats fast approaching. Two masked riders came into view, saw the stalled wagon and opened fire again. The bullets splintered parts of the wagon, but Lilly and Tommy remained safely on the wagon floor.

Sam aimed at the moving target, squeezed off a shot. The bullet grazed the shoulder of the rider on the right. He yelped in pain but did not stop. Both riders raced past the wagon, more interested in getting away than in continuing the fight.

Sam slipped out of the wagon and untied his horse. "I'm going after them," he said. "Can you make it the rest of the way home?"

"It's just a little up ahead," Lilly said. "You've helped us plenty. Don't you worry about us."

"I'll check on you later," Sam said as he put his foot in the stirrup.

"Be careful," Lilly said.

The two riders had taken off from the main road and were headed straight to the fishing camp Matt and Sam had set up.

"I'll be careful, but those two are the ones that need to worry," Sam said. "They're headed straight for Matt . . . and I think he might get kind of ornery when they interrupt his fishing!"

Chapter 6

Hardesty and Cooper had seen Sam face King Petty earlier in the day. They gave the stranger credit for having guts and a quick draw, but figured an ambush would be an easy matter. Things had gone wrong. Sam was not only still alive, but was now on their tails, and the two still weren't quite sure what went wrong.

"Damn, we should have had him," Hardesty, a tall red-haired man, yelled.

"I came close," Cooper said as he tried to keep his balance while his horse went up a small hill. He was slightly pudgy and now favored his left shoulder, which still stung from Sam's near-miss. "Would have had him if not for that lucky shot."

"Tell that to Petty. He won't accept that as an excuse."

"You tell it to Petty," Cooper continued. "I'm tempted to just skip this area. Anywhere would be safer than here when Petty gets riled."

"I'm not sure our friend will go along with that idea."

Cooper looked behind them and saw Sam riding

through the trees. Sam had wasted no time in going
after the two bushwhackers. After his quick goodbye
to Lilly and Tommy, he was racing after his attackers.
Sam didn't have to worry about trying to follow the
trail since they were not that far ahead of him and were
more interested in escaping than covering their tracks.

"The bastard is following us!" Cooper said.

"He's as crazy as Petty!"

"Doubt if he's as mean . . . but I don't intend to take
any chances!"

Hardesty pulled his rifle and shot at the figure chas-
ing him and Cooper. He missed by a wide margin. Sam
continued as if he hadn't even heard the shot.
Hardesty shot three more times, with the only result
being that he lost precious minutes from his head start.

Though the two riders rode fast, they could not stay
very far ahead of Sam, who had been on a horse
almost since birth. Sam quickly narrowed the gap to
the point where Hardesty and Cooper could almost
see Sam's dark eyes coming at them.

"Let's split up," Hardesty yelled. "He can't come
after both of us! Maybe we can get him in a crossfire!"

Hardesty went right and Cooper went left. Hardesty
looked back and saw Sam was following him! He shot
again. This time Sam returned the fire, though he also
missed.

Suddenly, Sam was gone. The outlaw stopped,
looked around cautiously, trying to figure out what he
should do next. He had only a few seconds to consider
before a large man on horseback exploded through the
trees, jumping gracefully and landing just a few hundred feet in front of him.

Hardesty, shocked, pulled back too far on his

horse's reins, causing it to buck. The tall outlaw held on and then kicked the horse to get it running again.

Sam gave chase, his horse following less than a dozen paces behind.

Cooper had just stopped his horse, allowing it to catch its breath, when Hardesty almost ran over him.

"He's behind me!" Hardesty yelled. "The bastard's behind me! Shoot him!"

Before Cooper could draw his gun, Sam had him pinned with a few shots of his own. It was all the convincing that Cooper needed. He spurred his horse away from Sam, joining Hardesty in a mad dash for safety, though the pudgy outlaw had a difficult time keeping up.

They rode for minutes that seemed like hours, headed for the creek, to possibly get to town and safety. Too late, they spotted the smoke and realized they were headed straight for somebody's camp.

Hardesty and Cooper looked behind them from the backs of their speeding horses, saw Sam wasn't about to give up, and realized they didn't have much choice in the matter.

They urged their horses to even greater speed, even though their path would take them right through the camp.

Lilly was as tired as she had ever been in her life. In a single day, she had lost her husband, buried him, and almost been raped and kidnapped by one of the worst men she had ever seen. If not for Sam Two-Wolves, she might now be . . . another victim of King Petty. It was almost more than a body could take. She felt drained, and was surprised she had any energy left at all.

Lilly was used to hard work, having been born and raised on a homestead. And she was used to death, having seen her father and brother die. Yet losing her husband was so unexpected and so sudden that the shock was far worse than anything she had ever known. She knew that the initial shock would be followed by pain, and that she would eventually get on with her life. In the meantime, she had to be strong for her and her son's sake.

Today she had taken some hesitant first steps for which she was proud, such as hitching and driving the wagon into town on her own. When Jack was alive, he had always handled those chores, and Lilly had been content to let him handle the reins. Now that Jack wasn't around, she would have to learn to do a lot more things on her own.

The horses were close enough to home that they now knew the way and needed little encouragement. They were eager to get to their barn and some fresh hay. Lilly held the reins loosely. Tommy sat on the seat beside her, eyes open but quiet.

"Why did he have to kill Daddy?" the boy asked. His voice could barely be heard above the creaking of the wagon.

Lilly put her hand on his shoulder, squeezed it. "I don't know. Some men are just plain mean. Who knows why they're that way? They just are."

"It's not fair."

"Life's not fair. We just got to do with what we have. The Lord helps those who help themselves."

"Do you like Sam?"

Lilly paused. "What kind of question is that?"

"I think Sam's going to help us."

"Maybe he will. He's just a stranger to us, but already has done more than anybody in town. Except for maybe the Ponders. But I wonder if they would have done as much if Sam hadn't been there, as well."

"Do you like him?"

"He seems to be a good man. Though he's a lot different than your daddy."

"Yeah. I suppose so." Tommy paused, then continued, "He really stood up to Petty, didn't he? And the way he took off after those men who shot at him!"

"He's quite brave . . . or foolhardy. I think any woman that catches him will have her hands full."

The horses paced into the barnyard and halted. Lilly wearily climbed down from the wagon and asked, "Tommy, would you unhitch the team and toss them some hay?"

"Sure, Mom."

The woman was so tired that she was almost to the door before she realized that two strange horses were tied at the side of the house. For a moment she froze, remembering the close call she'd had in town earlier in the day. She wished she had a gun in her hand, then realized that she had never learned to shoot one. The only guns Jack had owned were the rifle and a little revolver he'd kept in the nightstand by the bed. If Sam came by, she'd ask him to show her how to use them.

But that would be another day, if she lived through this night. She felt chilled as she climbed onto the porch and into the front room.

Marshal Holt and another man were seated in the chairs, feet outstretched, talking to themselves. Holt had the decency to at least stand when Lilly entered the room. The other man remained seated.

"Hello, ma'am," Holt said. "Hated to barge in on you like this, but we have some business to talk about."

Jack had kept a loaded shotgun on the wall. Lilly glanced at the rifle hanging over the door. It was still in place. She wondered if she could get to it and figure out how to use it in time to do her any good.

She said, "Marshal. I'm surprised to see you out here. To what do I owe this visit?" She was surprised at how calm her voice sounded.

Holt scratched himself and sat back down. "Well, I've been doing a lot of thinking," he said. "About what you and I talked about in town, that is."

"Before or after I was kidnapped?"

"It wasn't exactly a kidnapping." Holt stopped, remembered the words that Petty had used. "It was more of a . . . misunderstanding. I didn't really understand that you felt your husband was murdered and you wanted an investigation."

"I thought I made that very plain," Lilly said, feeling warmth come to her face and a chill to her voice. "And you've made your position very clear, as well. You work for Petty, and that's all there is to it. Now get out of my house."

"Just hold on, lady," Holt continued. "I agree that it's my job to look into such accusations. A leading citizen's been accused of a crime, and it's my duty to clear him. Or not."

"Get to the point, Marshal."

Holt cleared his throat.

"What I'm trying to say is that I'll be glad to conduct an investigation."

Lilly looked at him in disbelief.

"You? Conduct an investigation? What a laugh."

"But before I can open an investigation, I need some evidence," Holt continued. "Most important, I need the body. You'll need to dig up the body so that I can look it over, make sure he was shot like you said . . ."

Lilly reacted without thinking and in a way that was out of character for her. She crossed the floor in the blink of an eye and slapped Holt so hard that the crack filled the room. Holt had started to dodge another blow when a strong hand caught her arm.

"Settle down, widow," the second man said, leering down at her. "That's an officer of the law you're trying to hit."

Holt rubbed his face, where a red welt was starting to form.

"Thanks, Conn," he said. Then, to the woman, he added, "Hell, lady, that hurt!"

"How dare you come in here and demand that I desecrate my husband's body. He's dead and buried. I plan to let him rest in peace. Now get out of my house."

"This is official business," Holt said. "We need to investigate your allegations. Don't think we'll let you off so easily! We could get a court order, you know."

"Go to hell."

"Then you're willing to drop the charges?" Conn asked. "Marshal said it. No evidence, no investigation."

"I'm not going to let you do anything to my husband's body."

"Then that's it," Holt said, pushing himself out of the chair.

"The widow didn't say she'd drop the charges," Conn said. "Might be a good idea to see the body, anyway."

Tommy ran into the room, recognized Holt and Conn.

"What are these men doing to you, Mommy?" he demanded. "Are they bothering you?"

"No, son, they're just leaving."

Holt hurried awkwardly from the room. Conn went a little slow, brushing his tall body against Lilly.

"Just think about it," Conn whispered in her ear. "When Petty gets through with you, it'll be my turn."

Lilly tried to slap him, but he was already at the door. He grinned as he left and said, "Boy, if I were you, I'd also watch my step. Never know when something could happen to you, just like your daddy."

Matt was not seriously concerned, but he was wondering about Sam. It should have been a short trip to town, but by early evening Sam had not returned. Matt figured Sam could handle himself well enough, so had no plans to go looking for him. Sam would show up when he was good and ready.

Matt stretched, trying to work the kinks out of his bones. He had more aches and pains from a day that was supposed to be relaxing than he'd had from times when he had herded cattle all day or fought Indians. At least he had finally got some fishing done, and the air was now filled with the wonderful aromas of cooking fish and hush puppies.

Apparently the Browns were as good cooks as they had said.

Matt decided that maybe this would help to make up for some of the aches and pains that he had suffered as a result of the fight earlier in the day with Derrell. A good stack of fried fish could make lots of problems easier to handle.

Matt strolled over to the fire, where the elder Brown had his sleeves rolled up and was cooking the fish. He already had a panful and was cooking more.

"You said you expect your partner to be back pretty soon?" Lester Brown asked.

"Any minute now," Matt replied. "I expected him a long time ago, but he probably stopped for a beer."

"Has he got an appetite, as well?"

"Let me put it this way," Matt explained. "He could polish off what you have cooked here . . . and then be ready to settle in for some serious eating!"

"My kind of man!" Lester said. "We've got plenty. It should make him a happy man."

"If he doesn't get back soon, I'll just have to eat his share," Matt said. "It all looks and smells mighty good . . ."

Matt picked up a piece of fish that had been fried to a deep golden brown and almost had it to his mouth when two riders galloped out of the woods toward the creek. They almost knocked down Derrell, who was cooking some hush puppies over a separate fire.

Matt popped the fish into his mouth and pulled his gun. Before he could shoot, a third figure rode into the clearing.

"Sam! What in blazes is going on?"

Sam stopped in the middle of the clearing and untied some bags on his saddle.

"Long story." He tossed the bags to Matt. "Here are the supplies I went after. Planned to be back sooner, but I ran into a few little delays. I'll tell you later."

"Seems kind of rude, to not stay for supper," Matt said, conversationally. "Especially considering all the work we've gone through to make it!"

"I'll be back in time for supper!" Sam replied. "How many meals have you known me to miss?"

"Precious few," Matt admitted, saddling his own horse. "That's one thing I don't have to worry about with you. Though I thought you were going to stay out of trouble this time!"

"Good intentions, and all that!" Sam turned his horse and kicked it into motion. He slowed long enough to say to Lester, "That fish looks and smells damned good!" And then he was off again.

"That's Sam, my partner," Matt said as he put his hand on the saddle.

"Kind of thought so," Lester said.

"I'm going to help Sam," Matt explained. "Make yourselves at home. We'll be back by the time it's ready to eat!"

Chapter 7

Ralph Smiley enjoyed his job more and more every day. He sat easily on his horse on the side of the ridge, looking into the valley.

Another rider worked his way leisurely up the narrow trail until he was beside Smiley.

"Sure a pretty sight, isn't it?" Smiley said, rubbing his beard.

"Sure is," Ash Crawford answered. "In all the miles I've ridden, I don't think I've ever seen such a picture." He paused, then added, "That is, if you like cows."

He laughed and slapped his knees.

Smiley tried to ignore him, though that wasn't easy to do. Ash was over six feet tall—inches taller than Smiley—and outweighed Smiley by a good fifty pounds. He carried a big gun on his hip, tied low, and a Bowie knife in a holster strapped to his leg. He was a dangerous man, employed by King Petty to keep an eye on Smiley and the rustling operation. Ash was an aggravation, but putting up with him was a small price to pay since Smiley had no intention of ever crossing Petty.

At times, however, temptation seemed to beckon to him. Admiring the scene in the valley below him now was one of those times. The spring grass was a fresh, cool green. The cattle grazing were shades of velvety browns and blacks. A clear stream meandered through the middle of the valley. The sun was shining brightly, making everything look bright and new.

It looked like the ranch that Smiley had always wanted, but never had. Early in his life, circumstances had led him to a life of crime, rustling other people's cattle instead of raising his own. He was not particularly proud of his life, but most of the time did not think about roads not taken. He had to admit, however, that he had taken a liking to this valley and was starting to think about it as "his" valley.

"I know how you feel about cattle," Smiley said. "I don't know why Petty even bothers having you out here."

"He knows how much you like cows," Ash said. "You might get some ideas about cutting out some of the choice critters for your own use. He can't have you stealing his stolen cows, can he?"

This valley was exactly what Smiley would have picked out for himself, if he would have had the chance. Not only was it beautiful, but it was perfectly situated since it was a relatively short drive to the army fort a little farther north, where the government would buy all the beef they could get, no questions asked. A man could make a fortune here—legally. He was making even more for Petty—illegally. He could see how some men might be tempted to cheat a little bit, even though with Petty that would mean a quick execution or a slow, painful death, depending on the mood he was in at the time.

"No danger of my taking any of Petty's cattle," Smiley explained. "I'm a little too fond of living."

"If you call this living. I don't know what you see out here. Me? I'd rather be in town with Petty, drinking whiskey with a gal in my lap."

Down below, the cowboys working with Smiley pushed the new cattle taken from the Brown land into the group. These were good-looking animals, healthy and with just the right amount of fat on them.

"Why'd you come up here, Ash? I somehow doubt it was to discuss your social preferences."

Ash gestured to the animals below.

"Those are the cows you got from Brown and his son, right?"

"Yeah."

"Wanted to talk with you about the way you handled old man Brown today."

"I handled him."

"True. But you went awful easy on him. You could have shot him when you had the chance. But you let him go. That means he could come back. And next time he might have help."

"I doubt it. He wouldn't dare to take on any of us. Not as long as we're working for Petty."

Ash moved his horse closer to Smiley and poked him in the chest with his finger.

"Now get this straight. You work for Petty, you play by his rules. If Brown comes around again, you shoot him."

"That's not my job. I've killed men in my time. But I'm a rustler, not a killer."

"We don't want anything to go wrong. If you don't take care of Brown, then I will. And after I solve that problem, I'll shoot you. Got it?"

Smiley looked down at the valley for another minute, trying to keep his anger under control.

"I got it."

"Good." Ash started back down the hillside. "Enjoy the view."

Sam didn't have to look back to know that Matt was mounting his horse to join the chase. The two bushwhackers were making a valiant effort to escape, but they hadn't pulled very far ahead, even with Sam taking the time to stop and chat with Matt. They plunged into the creek where Matt had been fishing earlier and started to splash through the water.

Sam urged his horse into the water, as well, when Matt suddenly appeared from downstream in a path that would cut off the escape route.

Hardesty and Cooper looked at each other and spurred their horses faster. Matt pulled his Colt, placed two well-aimed shots near the heads of the bushwhackers. They halted in their tracks and reversed direction, splashing water all around them in their haste to get away.

Matt caught up with Sam and they gave chase, side by side.

"Thought I told you to stay out of trouble!" Matt said.

"So you did. Only, when did I ever listen to your advice?"

"Good point. But you should!"

"Then think how boring your life would be!"

The two blood brothers splashed up on shore, closing the gap between them and the bushwhackers.

"You think this is a good idea?" Matt asked. "They're headed back for the camp—without even being invited for supper!"

"Such bad manners! That's almost as bad as taking pot shots at me!"

Matt and Sam could see the two riders nearing the camp where Lester Brown and his son, Derrell, were cooking supper. Lester looked up, surprised, as Hardesty raced toward him.

"Oh, hell!" the outlaw yelled, jerking his horse's reins to guide him around the fire. The horse was still dripping creek water. It slid near the fire, splashing Brown, who was holding a long metal fork he was using to turn the fish. Brown yelled and struck out with the fork. It missed Hardesty's animal, but hit the rear of Cooper's horse with a loud smack.

The hot fork surprised the horse, causing it to take a leap forward, bumping the other animal and pushing it against the hot kettle. It whinnied and started to buck, kicking the pot, scattering hot coals and splashing grease and fish.

Brown started to curse. Sam and Matt arrived at the scene but were unable to stop the chaos.

Derrell barely got out of the way of the two horses that were jumping and kicking. The grease that had splashed onto the coals caught fire and blazed up, engulfing even the plates of food already fried.

Sam groaned. "Now they've really committed a crime!" he said. "They crash the party and then crash the food! They shouldn't have done that!"

"You'll just have to earn your keep . . . it's your turn to catch the fish this time!"

Sam gave a rebel yell and sprinted toward the mess. He leaped from his horse's back and grabbed Hardesty by the collar, pulling him from his bucking horse to the ground. Hardesty tried to punch Sam, but slipped in the grease. Sam's foot kicked a pot, which rattled across the ground. Derrell raced over, grabbed it and gracefully swung it against Hardesty's head. His eyes glazed over, and then he collapsed to the ground. His sleeve brushed against one of the coals, causing the cloth to scorch.

Cooper finally got his horse under control, but Brown wasn't going to let him get away, either. He grabbed the outlaw as he tried to ride away, pulled him from the saddle and hit him on the side of the head with the fork in his hand. Cooper staggered, turned in time to see Matt and Sam both facing him.

He stopped, but not fast enough.

"This is for shooting at me!" Sam said.

"And this is for messing up our supper!" Matt added.

Two fists punched out at the same time, hitting Cooper in the face.

He fell backward, sliding toward the creek through the flaming grease, igniting his shirt. Brown stepped over to Cooper and picked him up by the shirt.

"Should I?" he asked the two blood brothers.

"Guess we shouldn't let them burn, at least not before we have a chance to talk with them a little," Sam said. "Guess that wouldn't be a polite way to treat dinner guests."

"By all means, let's show our guests the same courtesy they showed us," Matt agreed.

Brown took Cooper and Derrell picked up Hardesty. They stepped toward the river and threw the outlaws into the water with a loud splash followed by a hiss of steam.

Lilly tried to look strong in front of her son, but it was a losing battle. After Marshal Holt and Conn had left, Lilly had barely moved from the spot where she had been standing. Tommy held her hand. He figured that with his father dead, he was the man of the family, but he didn't know how to fill that role. He held her hand, trying to think about what to do next. He had never seen his mother like this before, and it scared him.

The woman shivered and sat down on the easy chair in the front room. Too much had happened in too short of a time. Why was it happening to her? Twenty-four hours before, she had been a happily married woman whose main concern had been about how to best prepare supper for her husband. Now she was a widowed woman who not only had to deal with her grief and how to continue to work her homestead, but also had to worry about threats and harassment from King Petty and his men. Petty almost always got what he wanted, and now he apparently wanted her . . . and was willing to kill her husband and hurt her son to get her.

She shuddered again.

Tommy looked up at her, trying to be brave. It seemed Lilly couldn't stop shaking, but she had to try.

She clutched the arm of the chair and tried to think about the situation calmly. What could she do to protect herself?

"Tommy, you're going to have to be a man now, and I'm going to talk straight with you," Lilly said.

"Yes, Mom."

"Those men are after us. From now on we cannot assume that we will be safe. Not any place. Not any time. We know that the law will not help us. Nor can we assume that Sam . . . Mr. Two-Wolves . . . will be there to save us. I know this is very tough on you. I don't know how you've gotten through this day. But you're strong. I'm proud of you."

"What are we going to do?"

Lilly chewed on her lip as she thought. She had been used to Jack making all the decisions, but she had surprised herself a few minutes earlier when she'd reacted with uncharacteristic strength against Petty's men. Maybe it was time she started to make her own decisions, as well.

"First thing we must do is to be more careful. Those men were waiting for us inside our house and I walked right up to them. From now on, you and I will stay together. I'll help you do your chores, and you will help me do mine. Each of us will try to watch out for the other, and give warning at even a hint of danger. And we will make sure the doors and windows are locked. Let's take care of that now."

Lilly placed a chair against the door while Tommy closed the shutters. It would not stop a determined man from getting in, but at least it was action. And it might slow down an attack. Maybe it was false hope, but Lilly started breathing easier.

"Now what, Mom?" Tommy asked.

"Come with me."

Tommy followed his mother into the bedroom. She stopped by the nightstand, opened the drawer and pulled out the small revolver. She didn't know much about guns. She had never been interested, and since Jack hadn't liked guns, he hadn't explained much to her. Jack had used the gun mainly to shoot snakes and coyotes that got too near the house or livestock, so he had shown her how to load it and shoot it, though he'd asked her not to bother it.

"You ever shoot this thing?" Lilly asked.

"No. I wanted to. The other kids all have their own guns and know how to use them. But Dad . . ." He almost choked up, then continued. "But Dad said he didn't like guns. He never let me fool with it."

"That's going to change tomorrow. You and I are both going to learn how to shoot these guns. Maybe we could ask Sam to help show us how to use them. But no matter, we're going to protect ourselves one way or the other. I'm not going to allow what happened to your dad to happen to you." She found the box of bullets in the drawer. "Just in case . . . something happens . . . let me show you how to load this gun. I'll use the rifle."

She awkwardly opened the gun, removed the bullets and inserted fresh ones. Then she let Tommy do it several times. This could also be a false sense of security, but it made Lilly and her son feel better.

"This ain't so tough," Tommy said.

"You're just putting bullets in the gun. Don't get too sure of yourself or you may shoot yourself in the foot." She took the gun back, then placed it on the bed beside her. "And I don't want you getting any ideas about using this gun, or any other gun, to try and shoot Petty or his men. I want to keep you alive."

"But they won't get me . . ."

"Don't talk back." She looked around the room, trying to think of anything else she could do. "From now on, I also want us to sleep in the same room. I'll put some blankets on the floor in your room."

Tommy ran from the room. Lilly let him. He came back in with blankets and a pillow.

"No, Mom. You need your sleep. I'll sleep on the floor. And I'll try to watch the door."

"We both need our sleep. Today was the worst day of our lives. Tomorrow probably won't be much better."

"Don't worry, Mom. We'll face it."

Hardesty and Cooper woke with water in their eyes and mouths and pain in almost every bone in their bodies. They opened their eyes to see Sam, Matt, and the Browns standing over them, arms crossed, with angry looks in their eyes.

Cooper groaned as he felt blisters on his skin from the flames. He looked down and saw that while his shirt was burned and his chest was red, he was not seriously injured. He held his head as Hardesty said, "What are you going to do with us?"

Sam said, "What do you think? I know you're Petty's men. I know you tried to kill me."

"And look at all the damage you've done here!" Matt said. "You two are not what I'd consider sociable types."

"I get it. You two are going to talk us to death—"

Matt's fist lashed out suddenly, striking Hardesty and forcing his red-haired head back.

"We haven't decided not to kill you yet," Matt said. "I'd be a little more respectful if I were you."

"You could have killed us, if you wanted," Cooper said, not bothering to look up. "So you want something from us."

"Smart man," Sam said. "I think you two have learned your lesson . . . but I want your boss to also learn that there are some men he cannot control. Go back to Petty and tell him to not try anything like this again, or he will have to answer to Sam Two-Wolves."

Sam reached down, pulled both of the outlaws up by what was left of their shirts, and pushed them toward their horses.

"Now get out of here before I really lose my temper," Sam said.

Chapter 8

Though Matt was angry, he still had to smile as the two outlaws ignored their aches and pains, got back on their horses and raced out of the camp back to town. Sam could throw the fear of the devil in somebody if he wanted, because his threats were not empty. Hardesty and Cooper were lucky they were still alive.

"You're getting tender-hearted in your old age," Matt suggested. "You chase those two across hell's half acre; then you let them go."

"Needed a little sport," Sam answered. "Decided life was getting a little too dull."

"Nothing like getting shot at to spice things up some," Matt agreed. "I didn't much think you could go into town and *just* get a few supplies. I imagine you'll hear again from your new friends."

"And from their boss. That's why I wanted him to get the message."

Lester Brown shook his head and said, "You two boys sure take the cake. You act like getting shot at and beating the crap out of a couple of no-goods like that is just an everyday thing. You make jokes about it!"

"Yep," Matt said.

"You bet," Sam agreed.

Lester kicked at the remains of the fire and the overturned pot that had held the fish.

"One thing's for sure," he said. "The fight left quite a mess."

"And no supper," Sam said sadly. "I was looking forward to it."

"That's what you get for being late," Matt said. "Except I was looking forward to supper myself. Especially since I didn't have to cook it. Lester Brown here, and his son, Derrell, kindly agreed to do the cooking tonight. So much for the fish fry."

"Not much left here. Let's get this mess cleaned up. Then let's head on into town for some supper and a few beers. There's quite a bit I need to tell you."

"Brown has some interesting information, as well."

"Then come on. I'll buy everybody supper and the first round of drinks."

It didn't take long to pick up the pots and move the remaining supplies. The small group, led by Matt and Sam, arrived in the town of Snake Creek before dark. The men rode slowly down the dirt street, ignoring the whispered talk and the hard stares directed at them.

"Looks like your message was delivered," Brown said. "If I were you, Sam, I'd be a little concerned about what the answer might be."

"I always have an open mind, and am willing to discuss the situation," Sam said.

"I bet."

"He's a very reasonable man," Matt agreed. "Most of the time. Except when he gets mad."

Several men came out of the Black Bull Saloon as the group passed, but did not try to stop them.

"That's where King Petty hangs out," Brown explained. "Those are some more of his men. You two are asking for trouble."

"Not us. We never look for trouble. We just mind our own business. We're just innocent victims. Besides, you must not be too worried—you're still riding with us."

Derrell laughed and said, "Hell, you offered to buy us supper. Don't think we'd pass up a chance like that, do you?"

"At first I didn't much care for you two," Matt said. "Especially since you introduced yourself with a gun in your hand."

Sam laughed and said, "So that's how you all got hooked up, Matt? And you talk about *me* staying out of trouble!"

Matt ignored the comment and continued, "But I admit I was wrong. I'm liking you two better all the time."

Sam led the group past the saloon toward a small general store. He said, more seriously, "You already know I made some enemies this afternoon. I also made a few friends. I want to introduce you all. They might help to fill in a few gaps that I'm not even sure about yet."

Henry Ponder could not keep his mind on the work in front of him. He was supposed to be restocking shelves, but his mind kept wandering to the stranger who had ridden into town that afternoon, confronted King Petty, and lived to tell about it. Petty had terrorized the town for years, and nobody seemed to be able to do anything about it. Maybe Sam Two-Wolves had just gotten lucky. Or maybe he was just working on borrowed time. Henry was concerned that was the case, since nobody had successfully stood up to Petty and lived to tell about it.

"Henry?" He turned at Clarissa's voice. She was watching him with concerned eyes. As always, he felt warmth at the sight of her and wished he could have done more for her.

"Sorry. I didn't hear you walk in."

"You seemed lost in thought. I almost didn't want to disturb you."

"Glad you did." He put the can in his hand down on the counter. "I've been thinking about Sam Two-Wolves. He doesn't know what he's gotten himself into. It's tragic what happened to Jack Brandom and his family. It's heroic that Sam stepped in when he did. But I hate to see him wind up like all the others."

"And yet part of you hopes he comes back . . . to help. Nothing wrong with that."

Henry smiled sadly. "As always, you read me like a book."

"I think Sam will be back. There's something about him that sets him apart from other men. My grandfather called it the Warrior Spirit. It's what separates a true warrior from just a strong man . . . or a thug. Petty doesn't have it. Sam does. He'll be back."

"He'd be better off to just keep riding."

"It'd go against his grain. He'll fight because it's the

right thing to do. I wouldn't be surprised if we see Sam again very soon . . ."

"Do I hear my name spoken in vain?"

Henry and Clarissa both spun around in surprise to see Sam standing in the door with another man beside him. They could have been brothers, not just in appearance, but because they both seemed to generate the same strength.

"We were speaking about you, Sam," Clarissa said. "We were hoping you'd come back."

"How was the fishing?" Henry asked.

"Had a little excitement," Sam explained. "Didn't get a chance to do much fishing today, after all."

Matt laughed. "Hell, his friends that came to visit caused such a ruckus that Sam didn't even get a hook in the water! And they messed up our supper to boot. So he's going to buy us some. Know a good place here in town?"

Sam shook his head and stepped all the way inside. "This is my partner, Matt Bodine. Matt, this is Henry and Clarissa Ponder. They own this store and helped me out this afternoon." Lester and Derrell then stepped into the room. "This is—"

"Hi, Lester," Henry said. "How's the cattle business?"

"Not as good as yesterday. My luck finally ran out. Lost about a hundred head this morning."

"I see you all know each other," Sam said. "So I'll cut my introductions short. I am buying supper, though. You two want to join us?"

"You men go on," Clarissa said. "I'll close the store for the day."

Henry recommended a little restaurant owned by

Charlie Hacker. Matt and Sam nodded with approval as they entered. It was neat and clean, with checkered tablecloths and curtains on the windows. The aroma of steak and potatoes came from the kitchen area. Several people were in the room, but it was not crowded.

A robust older woman approached the table as the men pulled up chairs. She asked, "What'll it be today, Henry?"

"Start off with a round of beers, Lynn, then bring the food and keep it coming. Our new friend, Sam, is buying. That means you may actually get paid in real money tonight!"

"Don't know about that . . . don't know if Charlie's system can stand the shock!" She looked at Sam. "You're the fellow that faced King Petty this afternoon, aren't you?"

"Yeah."

"Thought so."

"Looks like you're famous," Matt said.

"The whole town's talking about it. Sam Two-Wolves, your money's no good here. Supper's on the house. Make yourself at home. Food will be out in a few minutes. If Charlie gets back in time, I'll let him know you're here. He'd like to meet you."

Lynn brought the beers, followed by steak and potatoes. The men ate in good-natured silence through several helpings and rounds of beers. Finally, Sam pushed himself back from the table and said, "Guess we've abused Lynn's hospitality long enough."

"Wasn't fish, but it was good," Matt agreed. "Now, let's hear about this mess you got yourself into, so I can figure out how to get you out of it."

"As always, you're all heart," Sam said, sipping his beer. "But I'm used to it by now. It started when I came to town to get my supplies. I stopped in at Ponder's store. He'll verify that I was as innocent as could be."

Henry, getting into the spirit of the talk, quickly agreed.

"Oh, yes, Matt, I can vouch for Sam. He wasn't looking for trouble. In fact, we talked about his planned fishing trip!"

Matt rolled his eyes to the ceiling and said, "Now I'm outnumbered!"

"But then I heard a commotion outside and I saw these thugs trying to manhandle a woman, Lilly Brandom, and her boy, Tommy. So I stepped outside to look into the situation."

"Is she pretty?"

"Very pretty. But that has nothing to do with my helping. Unfortunately, some of the thugs pulled guns on me and I had to kill them. Turns out that the woman's husband was killed in cold blood earlier in the day by a man called King Petty. She was just trying to get some help from the city marshal. Needless to say, she didn't succeed."

Matt became more somber as Sam continued to talk.

"So now King Petty is out for you. He sent those others after you. That they not only failed but were humiliated will probably make Petty even more angry."

"Jack Brandom, the man Petty killed, was just a poor homesteader," Ponder said. "He never looked for trouble or hurt anybody. Petty's killed a lot of people, but this may be the worst he's ever done. He's crazy, if you ask me. There's lots of people in town who've wanted to do something to stop him, but nobody can figure out how."

"Petty is also the reason my path crossed the Browns'," Matt continued. "Derrell apparently thought I was one of Petty's men who had apparently rustled some Brown cattle. He gave me a pretty good fight before Lester came along and helped us straighten it all out before somebody got killed."

Sam leaned forward and asked, "Do you know anything about the rustling operation?"

"Petty's in control, but he's got some other fellow actually working it," Brown said. "His name is Ralph Smiley. He apparently knows his cattle. He always cuts out the best of the herd. He has someplace in the hills where he keeps them, and probably sells them up north. It's just like a regular business to him, since nobody's going to cross him. Not as long as he's with Petty."

Sam glanced at Matt. "Ralph Smiley . . . we've heard his name in connection with other cattle rustling operations, though he's stayed clear of us. Looks like he's found a good thing down here."

"Maybe. Except that I'm not sure being hooked up with a man like King Petty is ever a good thing."

"I couldn't just let Smiley and his men take my cattle without a fight," Lester continued. "So I followed and found Smiley, for all the good it did me. He laughed in my face and told me to get lost. I suppose I could have fought him, but I was outnumbered and outgunned."

"You don't sound defeated," Matt said. "You going to try and get your cattle back?"

"I haven't worked this land for twenty years just to give up now. Derrell and I will think of something."

Sam took another sip of beer. "Are you thinking what I'm thinking, Matt?"

Matt sighed and leaned back in his chair. "Yes, I suppose so. I didn't volunteer to help the Browns at first because I wanted to get some fishing in. But since those plans have changed . . ."

"I couldn't very well leave Lilly and Tommy to the mercy of Petty, in any case. And now Petty is looking for a fight. He sent those two clowns after me, and somebody trying to kill me is not something I take to kindly."

"So why not bring the fight to him . . . and at the same time help our new friends, the Browns?" Matt concluded. "It's been a while since I've punched cows, and it's about time I reacquainted myself with the critters. How'd you boys like to go on a little cattle drive?"

Brown smiled and said, "I'd be delighted!"

"Let's do a little planning," Matt said. "I'd like to look around a little more, to see what we're up against."

"We're with you, whatever you decide," Lester said.

Ponder cleared his throat and said hesitantly, "Count me in, too. If there's anything I can do."

Chapter 9

Petty was at his usual table when Hardesty and Cooper sheepishly walked in. The moved slowly, as if they were in pain. Holt, standing at the bar, started to smirk.

"Go ahead and laugh, you fool, and I'll kill you," Hardesty said to the marshal. "I don't care who you think you are."

Holt turned his attention back to his beer, but said under his breath, "Looks like Sam Two-Wolves strikes again."

Petty looked up and growled, "What the hell happened to you two?"

"Well, Two-Wolves was a little tougher than we had thought . . ."

"Did you kill him?"

The two outlaws scraped their boots on the floor.

"We had an ambush all set up, but something happened . . . ," Cooper said.

"Answer me. Is Sam Two-Wolves dead?"

"No . . . no. He did have a message for you. He said for you not to try anything against him again, or—"

Petty jumped up and turned the table over with a loud crash. The glasses and bottles fell and broke on the sawdust floor. He punched Hardesty in the gut, doubling him over in pain, then pivoted and kicked Cooper in the groin.

"Look at you two," Petty said. "Send you out for a simple job, and you come back with your tails between your legs. Looks like he cleaned up the countryside with you." He spit. "Damned, you're piss poor excuses for men."

"But he had help," Cooper groaned, trying to stand. "He had another guy with him, just about as tough as he was—"

Petty's boot tip lashed out, hitting Cooper in the chin, snapping his head back. The thug hit the floor, groaning louder than ever.

"I don't want excuses. I hate excuses. I hate people getting in my way. You understand?"

Conn, standing at the door, called out to Petty. "Hey, speak of the devil . . . here comes that SOB now. He's acting like he owns the town, just riding in as pretty as you please!"

Petty stepped over the two men in pain on the floor to look down the street.

"Well, that's interesting," Petty said. "Looks like Two-Wolves has himself some friends."

"The old guy is Lester Brown, a small-time rancher," Conn explained. "The one beside him is his son, Derrell. Guessing the third guy is Matt Bodine."

"How'd you know that?" Holt asked, stretching his neck to see over the other men without disturbing them.

"Somebody's got to keep on top of things," Conn

answered. "I've been asking around. Some of the boys know about Sam Two-Wolves and Matt Bodine. They've got themselves a reputation as troublemakers and gunfighters. King, you know how fast Two-Wolves is—you saw him in action. I've heard Bodine is just as fast or faster." Conn saw Petty scowling, so quickly added, "Course, neither is as fast as you, King. You can bet all kinds of money on that."

Petty stayed inside as the group passed by, thinking about what he should do about this new development. He wasn't worried. The idea of somebody actually being better than him never crossed his mind. But he was getting the idea that these two could cause him more trouble than he had originally expected. He watched as Sam led the group down the street straight toward Ponder's store.

"Looks like he's got another friend," Conn said. "My guess is that Henry Ponder has sided with him, as well. Two-Wolves has been a busy man for not being in town any longer than he has."

"You've done good," Petty said. "Keep on top of things."

He turned as some of his men flipped his table back upright and brought him a fresh bottle.

"You two, get out of my sight," Petty said to Hardesty and Cooper. "Don't come back until you do something right. I kind of think that'll be more than you can handle." The two men tried to stand. "Help that trash out of here."

Strong hands lifted the men and carried them toward the rear exit. Holt headed for the bar, when Petty's voice stopped him.

"Marshal Holt. It's time you started to earn your keep, as well."

"But, King, I went out to that widow woman's, like you said. I done my job."

Petty laughed. "Yeah, I bet you and Conn put some fear into that woman and boy," he said. "But I want you to do something else. Find out what Sam Two-Wolves and Matt Bodine are up to. Use your authority—such as it is. Go ahead and mess with them if you can."

Holt cleared his throat.

"That might be easier said than done . . ."

"If it don't get done, you might wind up in worse shape than Hardesty and Cooper."

"So what do you want me to do?"

"You're the marshal. You think of something."

Holt gulped the last of his beer and tucked his shirt back in his pants. "You coming, Conn?"

"Naw. You're on your own this time."

Suddenly his job didn't seem as much fun as it had, though it was a little late to quit now.

Matt and Sam pushed themselves away from the table at about the same time.

"Hey, Lynn, the apple pie was great!" Sam called out. "We'll be back later. Be sure to keep some for us!"

A tall man stepped out from the kitchen beside Lynn. "For you, we'll keep the whole pie," he said, holding out his hand. "My name's Charlie Hacker, and I'm glad to meet you. Just got in from a business trip, arranging for some supplies. My wife said you were here. Glad you came in. Heard how you faced King Petty this afternoon. Took a lot of guts."

"The toughest part is still to come, I think," Sam said. "But, thanks. My compliments to your wife. She's a helluva cook."

"That she is," Charlie agreed.

A man opened the door and stepped inside.

"Hello, Marshal," Charlie said. "What brings you here? I could give you some free coffee . . . but I know you usually stick to alcohol."

"I wanted to . . . have a talk with these strangers," Holt said. "I don't like roughnecks shooting up my town."

Sam's eyes grew hard, and he started to stand. Holt took a half-step back and continued, "You strangers look like trouble. The rest of you boys had better take warning. If I have to run them in, I might bring you all in, as well . . ."

Matt then stood up to his full height beside Sam. Holt took another half-step back.

Charlie said, "Don't go making empty threats, Holt. We all know you're just following orders."

"No, let him talk," Ponder suggested. "Let's hear what the marshal has to say."

Holt cleared his throat. "All right. I was blowing hot air. I admit it. But this is on the straight. Charlie, Henry, I've known you two all our lives. Though you've never liked me much, I feel I owe you a fair warning. King ain't too pleased with the way things are going, and that's the truth. He'll kill these two, even if they are supposed to be top guns. You know he will. And if you hang around with them, he'll probably also kill you."

"That warning may be the only decent thing you've done since we allowed you to take office—at Petty's insistence," Ponder said.

"Doesn't it scare you?" Holt asked. "You've all seen what Petty can do. You know what he's trying to do with that widow woman, harassing her like that—"

Sam's hand suddenly snatched Holt's shirt and pulled him across the table to him.

"What's he doing to the woman?"

"I didn't say anything. I didn't do anything. Just leave me alone . . ."

Sam lifted the portly man off the ground and said, "As a general rule, I try not to beat up on pathetic little men such as you, but I can make the exception. What's going on with Lilly?"

"We just paid her a little visit, is all," Holt said. "We didn't touch her or anything. Nobody would dare do that unless King gave the go-ahead, and he has his eyes on her—"

Sam threw Holt to the floor. He landed on his feet, stumbled, but remained standing.

"Don't say anything to King about this, would you? He sent me over here to scare you. If he knew I failed like those other two did . . ."

"So he got my message?" Sam asked.

"He got it."

Ponder laughed. "Not likely any of us are going to be having dinner conversation with Petty anytime soon. Why don't you tell him that you did your job."

"He won't believe me," Holt said. "Hell, I'm beginning to wish I never took this job."

"You can always quit," Charlie said. "There's still

some of us on the town council that'd be willing to hire a big gun to come in and clean up the town."

"Nope. I don't think King would let me quit. But believe me, this job is getting too dangerous for my health. I'd quit if I could. If I were you, I wouldn't talk much about those ideas of bringing in somebody to get rid of Petty. He doesn't need much reason to kill you."

Holt hitched up his pants and tried to swagger out.

"Kind of sad, isn't it?" Matt said, when Holt was out of hearing range down the street.

"He used to be the town drunk," Charlie said. "Petty picking him for marshal was his way of thumbing his nose at us . . . as if all the murder and mayhem he committed wasn't enough."

"Hope he stays out of the way when the shooting starts again," Matt said. "Don't think he'd last very long in a real fight." He turned to Sam and continued, "Think maybe we should pay a visit to your friend and her son?"

"The sooner, the better," Sam agreed. "I don't much like Holt's talk."

"We'll figure out tomorrow what to do about Brown's cattle," Matt suggested as he pulled and checked his gun.

"Thanks for the meal, Charlie," Sam said, tipping his hat. "Next time, we'll pay."

"When are you coming back?"

"Do you serve breakfast?" Matt grinned.

After Matt and Sam had left, the others remained sitting around the table, talking among themselves.

"Those two are quite a pair," Charlie said. "Sam's

already stood up to Petty. Matt looks like he'd be willing. Think they'd be interested in official jobs?"

"You mean like replacing Holt with Matt or Sam?" Ponder said. "A nice thought, but I don't know if they'd be interested or not. I imagine they've done some law officer work in their day, though they don't look like the usual lawman material. I know they would never run from a fight."

"They're hard to figure," Lester agreed. "Maybe they have their own code that they follow. Matt seemed hesitant to help me and Derrell at first, but now I think he's scrapping for a fight with Petty. Sam and Matt beat the crap out of King's men that shot at them. But Derrell also had a brawl with Matt, and now he acts like we're long-lost friends. I'm not sure what to make of them."

"Of course, we did apologize and offered to fry up some fish for them," Derrell suggested.

Ponder laughed. "Hell, maybe that's the secret! If we want to hire one of those boys, don't offer them money or appeal to their nobler instincts! Instead, give them all of Lynn's cooking they want! That might keep them around town for a while!"

Lester also laughed. "You know, that's crazy enough it might just work!"

Sam and Matt were always careful no matter where they travelled, but now their senses were even more alert than usual. They knew they had challenged Petty and that the killer would want to add their notches to his gun. As always, though, they rode easily, as if they hadn't a care in the world.

"Do you think we're a little on the crazy side?" Matt asked.

"No doubt of it," Sam agreed. "Especially in your case."

"You get us into this mess and you can say that about me?"

"Well, look at it logically. You give up a perfectly good fishing day to wrestle a bull . . ." Sam laughed and slapped his knee. "I sure as hell would have liked to have seen that! And then you become friends with a fellow that at first tried to beat the crap out of you, and now you offer to chase down some rustlers! Does any of that make any sense?"

"At least the Browns fried up supper for us . . . until you made your dramatic entrance!"

"True." Sam tipped his hat back and looked at Matt. "On the other hand, the person I helped is at least a pretty woman!"

"You do have me there!" Matt admitted. Then, more seriously, he added, "We've run across a lot of hard cases in our time, but sounds like this King Petty is about as bad as they come. These people really do need our help."

"I agree. A person would have to be a little crazy to get involved. But nobody ever said we had good sense!"

"It helps keep life interesting."

The two blood brothers rode quickly, though they did not seem to hurry. Matt and Sam noticed the green grass, the clear creeks, the fields that had started to be plowed.

"This is some decent land," Matt observed. "I'd rather run cattle than farm it, but to each his own. This area could handle just about anything you want to do."

"I think this is Brandom land," Sam said. "I only rode Lilly part of the way home. I probably should have made sure she was safe . . ."

Matt and Sam stopped abruptly as they came to the top of a small hill where a freshly dug grave overlooked a farmhouse. It could have been a pretty picture, with the house and trees in the front yard under the stars. The grave, however, was a grim reminder of the troubles facing the woman and her son.

The house was dark. No movement could be seen anywhere, not even in the barn.

"Maybe they're sleeping," Matt said. "Holt said they didn't hurt her."

"They could have come back," Sam said grimly.

"Let's separate and move in—" Matt started to say, but was interrupted when a shot exploded and whistled past his ear.

Chapter 10

The echo of the shot hadn't faded away before Matt and Sam went into action. They worked together as a well-practiced team, each instinctively knowing what to do.

Matt jumped to the ground, pulled his Colt, and rolled to the right. Sam scanned the area as he slipped to the ground and rolled to the left.

"Don't shoot," Sam warned.

"Why not?"

Another shot was fired, but missed its mark by an even wider margin than before.

"The shots are coming from the house," Sam said.

"Not a very good shot," Matt suggested.

"Exactly. It's probably Lilly. She saw us out here and got spooked. Petty's men would be a little more enthusiastic in their attack."

"Sounds reasonable. I'm getting a little tired of being shot at, but I can't blame the woman for shooting first and asking questions later. Not with her husband just getting killed and being threatened by the likes of Petty and his men. Have to give her credit for paying attention and not giving up."

"Wait here for a few minutes. I don't think anybody else is around, but you might want to keep watch, just in case."

"You got it."

Sam seemed to blend in with the darkness. Even Matt, whose wilderness skills were almost as good as Sam's, had difficulty keeping track of him. Sam moved close to the house where he could be seen from the window when he chose to show himself. For the moment, he had situated himself behind a huge oak tree in the front yard so that one of Lilly's wild shots wouldn't accidentally hit him.

"Lilly! Don't shoot! It's Sam!"

The voice from inside the house was faint, but the words were plain: "Sam! I'm coming out!"

Sam stepped out from behind the tree in plain sight as the door opened. Lilly came running out, still holding the gun, followed by Tommy. She hugged Sam.

"Are you all right?" he asked.

"Yes. Some of Petty's men came out and threatened us. They were horrible! But they didn't hurt us. Yet. I found my husband's gun, but I wasn't even sure how to use it. I saw somebody out there and I shot . . . oh, I could have killed you! I'm so sorry!"

"You did the right thing. When you're attacked, you defend yourself. Simple as that."

"Are you here to stay?" Tommy asked.

"For a while. I'd like you to meet somebody." Sam motioned, and Matt walked down the hill, leading his and Sam's horses. "This is my partner, Matt Bodine."

Lilly let go of Sam and held out her hand to Matt.

She was still concerned, but her eyes sparkled a little as Matt took her hand in his.

"Glad to make your acquaintance, ma'am."

"I'm sorry I shot at you," she said.

"Don't worry about it. Sam told me you were a strong and beautiful woman. He told the truth. I have a lot of respect for you. It's not often you find a woman with both strength and beauty."

Lilly allowed Matt to continue to hold her hand in his and smiled self-consciously.

"You're very kind. Thank you."

Sam smiled and slightly shook his head. Matt could be very charming when he wanted. Even he could not take away the woman's grief, but he could put a tiny sparkle in her eye in the midst of her fear.

"Would you all come in for some coffee?" Lilly asked.

"Thank you. That would be fine."

Matt handed the reins of the horses to Sam as he walked into the house with Lilly.

Though she had known Sam for only a few hours, he made her feel safe. And his partner, Matt, seemed just as competent and, if anything, was even more charming than Sam. Nothing could take away the pain she felt, but for a few moments she allowed herself the luxury of losing herself in Sam's businesslike strength and Matt's attentions. For the moment, it was the only comfort she had.

She went into the kitchen, built up the fire in the stove, and filled the coffeepot with water. As the pot heated up, she sat wearily at the table, put her hand on her arm, and promptly fell into a deep and dreamless sleep.

* * *

King Petty was getting damned tired of the idiots he had working for him. He knew that eventually he would have to face Sam, one-to-one, and kill him. However, he did expect more than he was getting from his men. They couldn't even make a threat stick!

Marshal Holt coming back into the saloon didn't help matters any. The joke was wearing thin.

"What is it, Holt?"

"I had a little talk with Two-Wolves and Bodine. And the others. I told them to back up. Or else."

"Good. And what happened?"

"They acted a little . . . upset."

Petty gulped down his drink and glared at the marshal.

"You know what, Holt? I don't like you. I never did like you. You're nothing but a weak drunk. A joke."

Holt stood uneasily.

"I do the best I can," Holt said, hoping his words wouldn't cause Petty to lose his temper.

"I've thought of a good punishment for all you weaklings. First thing tomorrow, take those other two clowns out to the Brandom place. Try to make good your threat to the woman."

"But . . . there's no need to dig up the body. We know that you killed Brandom . . . in self-defense. If you want the woman, why don't you just take her. What's the use of torturing her that way?"

"Because I want to bother the woman just for the hell of it. Because it will bother Two-Wolves. Because maybe Two-Wolves will kill all of you and save me the trouble. The reasons aren't any concern of yours. Are you arguing with me?"

"No . . . I'd never argue with you. I'll find the others. We'll take care of it."

"Tomorrow morning. Now get out of my sight."

In the front room, Matt and Sam talked quietly among themselves. Tommy was sitting in an easy chair, sleeping.

"The poor woman and kid are exhausted," Matt said. "They've been going on sheer guts."

"It is amazing," Sam said. "But weren't you spreading it on a little thick back there—even for you?"

"Not really. The woman's hurting. I gave her a few compliments—which were sincere, by the way—to make her feel a little better. I think she deserves at least that much."

In the chair, Tommy snored slightly.

"Fair enough. But now let's get back to business. You check out the house, make sure it's secure. I'll check out the barn and the rest of the area. Then we'll let these two get some sleep."

"Sounds good."

Matt started to the kitchen and called out to Sam before he even got to the front door.

"Take a look at this," Matt whispered, pointing out the woman sleeping at the table while the coffee boiled on the stove.

"Let's get them to bed. We can take turns guarding the house."

Matt reached down and picked up Lilly in his arms as if she were a child. She murmured something, but did not wake up. Matt carried her into the other room and put her on the bed. Sam did the same for Tommy, but put him on his blanket on the floor.

"How do we get into these situations?" Matt asked.

"Guess we just lead charmed lives."

"At least we got plenty of coffee. I doubt if King's men will be back tonight, but at least these two will be able to get a little sleep."

Cooper still hurt. He didn't know which was worse, the kick he had received from Petty or the punches from Matt and Sam. He walked carefully and placed his broad body on a stump. Hardesty sipped from a bottle and then slipped it to Cooper.

"Here. This will help."

"I'm not sure anything will help. Damned." The back of the Black Bull Saloon could be seen several hundred feet away. The door occasionally opened and closed, casting squares of light in the darkness. "Can you believe the way Petty treated us?"

"Lucky he didn't kill us. I still say we should have ridden away when we had the chance." Hardesty took the bottle back and took another sip.

"He didn't expect Two-Wolves to be so tough, either. Hell, it's like he ain't human or something."

"He's got senses like an Injun. He seemed to know where we were before we did. Damned."

The bottle passed back and forth.

"Well, we need to do something," Cooper said.

"Yeah. Like what?"

"Let's try again. And this time do it right."

"You're crazy. You want to face Two-Wolves and Bodine again?"

"You want to face Petty?"

"You have a point."

"How do we do that?"

"Don't you two have anything better to do than sit around and drink?" The two turned as Holt stumbled up to join them.

"Can you think of anything better?"

"Hell, no. So pass me the bottle!"

Holt took a gulp and passed it back. "Bad news," Holt said. "King's been thinking again. He's got another job for us to do. He wants us to finish the job Conn and me started."

The two outlaws groaned as Holt explained the plan to harass the widow.

"Is King crazy?" Cooper asked.

"Of course," Hardesty said. "But I'm not going to call him on it!"

"This could be our chance to fix things up."

Chapter 11

Sam had taken the first shift and Matt the second.
Even so, Sam had gotten up long before dawn and
joined Matt in the kitchen. He reached for the coffeepot, poured himself a cup and sat at the table with
Matt.

"A quiet night," Matt said.

"Thank goodness for that. At least for the sake of
Lilly and the boy. They've been through a lot."

"I've been thinking about this during the night,"
Matt continued. "About the best way to handle this
situation. Lilly and Tommy are basically alone. A mad
killer is after them. The best and easiest way to deal
with this is just to go into town and take out the
problem."

"True. But that creates another problem, doesn't it?
You don't believe in killing in cold blood—no matter
how much it is deserved. But we can't just leave the
family here without protection."

"At the same time, neither one of us can really
afford to stay here and guard the family indefinitely."

"Quite a problem," Sam agreed. "And if King Petty

is like most of his type, he won't be too anxious to face us, man to man. His kind are always tough as long as they have the upper hand. But let somebody face them who might be as good or better than they are and they turn tails and run."

"We bring the fight to him. We've got plenty of help on that one."

"So we will. Of course, there's no guarantee Petty will be in on that escapade. If he senses trouble, he'll probably stay clear."

"Or we might flush him out. Never know until you try."

"And in the meantime we need to do something about Lilly and Tommy."

"I'd suggest the first thing is to teach Lilly a little more about shooting."

"Are you volunteering?"

"Of course." Matt grinned. "I'm always willing to help a damsel in distress."

"Especially a pretty one."

"You know me better than that. I'd never take advantage of a person who is hurting like she is. But a man would have to be blind to ignore the fact that she is a bright and pretty woman. There's nothing wrong with that."

"No. I suppose not. You do have something of the white knight in you."

"Is that a compliment or an insult?"

"Take it any way you wish."

"Unfortunately, it is a quality I think we both share."

"It gets us in trouble."

"But you meet so many interesting people that way!"

Sam chuckled. "So you do."

"Helping Lilly learn to shoot is a simple thing, but it might make a difference."

"Good morning," Lilly said. Matt and Sam stood as the woman entered. Lilly seemed surprised at their action. She smiled and walked over to the stove. "Let me make you all some fresh coffee so you can have something to drink while I make the biscuits. You all haven't been up all night, have you?"

"One of us has," Sam said. "We thought it might be for the best. At least for the one night."

"There's no way I can thank you," Lilly continued. "This whole thing has me totally lost. I was so . . . frightened . . ."

"With good reason," Matt said. "To be honest, I don't know how you all are holding up as well as you are."

"It just doesn't seem real. One minute, Jack's alive and we're a family . . . and the next . . . he's gone . . ." It looked for a second like Lilly would start to cry again, but she found some strength from somewhere inside herself. She turned to her biscuits. "I'm still in a state of shock. I was so tired last night I don't even remember going to bed. Last thing I know, we were talking to you all, and then it was morning."

"Even at that you didn't get much sleep."

"We're still feeling better."

"How's Tommy?" Sam asked.

"He's outside doing his chores now."

Sam nodded. "Think I'll slip outside to see how he's getting along. If you don't mind."

"Do whatever you think is best. I trust you and Matt completely. As long as you get back in time for breakfast."

"Thanks. Wouldn't miss it for the world. I'll be back in a little while."

"Don't hurry too fast," Matt said. "That'll leave more breakfast for me!"

"Don't you wish!"

Lilly poured Matt a fresh cup of coffee, then prepared the biscuits for baking. Matt leaned back in his chair, sipped his coffee, and watched the woman work. She was pretty, but she also had an easy way about her in the kitchen. Her movements were graceful and efficient.

The domestic scene unsettled Matt a little. He was used to camping in the wilderness or eating in saloons and restaurants where the meals were often interrupted by fights. For a minute, he tried to imagine himself giving up a life of wandering and excitement in favor of a home and family such as this. At this moment, the choice was tempting . . . if there could ever be such a woman for him. Lilly was pretty, and there seemed to be some attraction, but some spark seemed to be missing. Matt wondered again, however, if he would ever be able to give up his life of adventure even if a woman like Lilly came along and the spark was there. It was not the first time Matt had considered the question, and it wouldn't be the last.

"Matt, I have a question."

"Shoot."

"Sam didn't really go out to help Tommy, did he? He really went out to make sure he wasn't in any danger."

"You're a smart woman, Lilly. Sam is a careful man."

"Why are you two doing this? I mean, it's not your fight. Sam risked his life yesterday for me even though he had never seen me before and had no idea who I was. Now you're here with him, helping us as if we were family or something. And from what I can tell, you've made a terrible enemy in King Petty. You've put yourself at great risk. It doesn't make any sense."

"I guess the easiest answer to that question is simply that we wanted to."

She shook her head and brought the biscuits from the oven. Matt noted that they were brown and looked delicious.

"I've always prided myself on my biscuits," Lilly said as she put them on the table. "Jack always liked them . . ."

"I'll be honest with you, Lilly. You and your son are in a lot of trouble, through no fault of your own. Sam and I will be in the area for a while, and will try to keep an eye on you, but we can't be here all the time. You showed a lot of spunk last night, but your aim was way off. I like to think I know a little about shooting, and I'd be pleased if you'd let me show you a few tricks."

"When would you want to do that?"

"The sooner the better. How about after breakfast?"

"I don't like guns. When Jack was alive we never had much to do with them. Things are different now. Sure. I'll give it a try."

"Good. Now, how about some of those biscuits . . ."

Lilly put her hands on her hips and gave him a hard look.

"Er . . . after you call in Sam to join us for breakfast, of course!"

Sam found Tommy in the barn throwing hay to the livestock. He slipped quietly inside, blended into the shadows and watched the boy work without being noticed. Tommy had a solemn look on his face, but not one of fear. The boy seemed to be listening to the sounds outside the barn, but continued his work at a steady pace. Sam noted with approval that the boy completed his tasks without cutting corners.

Sam cleared his throat and made a lot of noise as he entered the barn the rest of the way.

"Good morning, Tommy. Getting your chores done?"

"Like every morning. At least that hasn't changed."

"With your daddy gone, you'll probably be doing even more of a man's work than before."

"Expect so. Me and my mom will handle it."

"You will. It won't be easy."

Tommy paused in his work, leaned against the pitchfork. "Sam, would you teach me how to shoot?"

"I don't know. I suppose your mom would have a lot to say about that. I think Matt is going to teach her a little. She's the adult, so it makes sense that she'd be the one to learn."

"But I want to learn, too. My dad never liked guns, never let me even shoot one. The other kids grew up on guns. But not me. And now he's dead because of it. If he had been more like you, he'd still be alive . . ."

Sam stepped forward and grabbed Tommy by the shoulder. He was a little rougher than he intended, but the boy did not protest.

"I need to tell you something about your daddy," Sam said. "I never knew him. I never even met him. But I can tell you something about him. He was a good man, who did the best he could for you and your mom. He built up this homestead of yours into something good and productive. Don't you ever fault him for that. Don't you ever turn your back on what he taught you."

"But what'd he teach me? To just roll over and play dead?"

"I know he didn't die a coward's death. I know he faced King Petty's gun as a man, with bravery and courage. That's not something you get from a gun. As to what he taught you . . . son, you may not know that for many years. As you grow, you'll remember some of the things he said and the way he lived, and you'll use them. Then you'll know."

Sam let go of the boy. He looked up at Sam with a curious look.

"And how do you know so much about it?"

"I lost my own father, many years ago. I know he died as a brave man, because I saw him die. I could do nothing about it, because I made a promise to him . . . a promise that I am now keeping, and will keep until I die. Sometimes I wonder what I learned from him, since the life I'm now living is so much different than how I started out."

"I don't understand," Tommy said.

"The point is you have to honor your father and his wishes . . . even as you follow your own path. And you need to remember there are all kinds of bravery and heroism, and none of them come from the barrel of a gun. Men like King Petty may get their way through force and mistake that for courage. Don't you ever make that mistake."

Tommy gulped. "All right. Sam. I'll remember."

"I also don't want to hear any more bad talk about your daddy."

"I'll do what you say, Sam. But I still want to know . . . will you teach me to shoot?"

"We'll talk to your mom about it." From the house came Lilly's voice, calling Sam and the boy to breakfast. "After breakfast."

It was an informal meeting of the town council at Charlie Hacker's restaurant because it was still not safe to do much without King Petty's knowledge and approval. The group met early, before normal business hours, and hoped that nobody noticed the lights on earlier than usual.

"I'm willing to approach them with the offer," Charlie said. "As long as they're sticking around, they ought to have the power of the law on their side."

"Sam or Matt?" Lester asked. Though he and Derrell weren't actually citizens in the town of Snake Creek, they were considered friends of the blood brothers, so their opinions were valued.

"Either one would do."

Henry Ponder spoke up. "I suggest approaching Matt. From what little I know, I suspect he would be the more likely to take the job. Sam seems to be taking a more personal interest in the situation."

"Either way, we're playing with fire just talking about this," Charlie said. "If Petty found out, he might just shoot each of us for the fun of it. Or worse. Who knows what he might do if we actually fire Holt? And appoint Matt?"

"I think we're all just about dead, anyway," Ponder protested. "The longer Petty's allowed free rein, the more harm he's going to do. He's killed lots of people in the past, but murdering Jack Brandom was just too much. Jack always minded his own business. He was a family man. He had no enemies that I know about. Think about it. If Petty can kill him in cold blood and get away with it, the rest of us could be next no matter what we do. Petty just keeps getting meaner, crazier, and getting more and more men working with him. If we don't stop him now, there never will be any stopping him."

The others nodded their heads in agreement.

Charlie took a deep breath and said, "So it's decided. We'll fire Holt and hire Matt. As soon as he agrees to take the job."

"Now, the question is who has the guts to find Matt and offer him the job."

"I'll volunteer," Derrell said. The others looked at him curiously. "I've seen Matt in action. Don't forget, my first introduction to him was fighting him! I have a lot of respect for him, but I'm not afraid of him. I'll talk with him."

"I'll go along," Lester said. "He's already offered to help us get our cattle back. If we can talk him into pinning on a badge, maybe it'll increase the odds slightly in his favor."

"Or make him a target, like the others before him," Charlie said.

"Matt's not like the others," Ponder said. "He's not likely to allow himself to get shot in the back or bought off. And I'd lay odds that not even King Petty can outdraw him. I can't see Matt Bodine being buried in boot hill."

"Derrell, you're the man," Ponder said. "We are authorizing you to offer the position of City Marshal to Matthew Bodine, effective immediately upon his acceptance. Once he takes office, we'll not question his judgment or try to tell him how to do his job. We'll give him free rein to do the job, no matter what it takes."

Derrell stood, and put on his hat.

Charlie added, "And tell him if he takes the job, he can have as many meals here as he wants . . . on the house!"

Chapter 12

Matt held Lilly's hand in his as he showed her how to hold the revolver. The experience was pleasant enough, for her hand was long, slender, very feminine. Matt, however, kept his mind on the business at hand.

"Don't hold the gun so tightly," Matt explained. "It's not going to run away from you. And it's not going to turn on you. Just relax a little. Hold it securely, not stiffly."

"Like this?" Lilly asked, loosening her grip slightly.

"Yes. You're a fast learner. Now, give it a shot."

Lilly's gun was an older model .38, but it would do the job at close range. Matt had cleaned it up and adjusted it for her. Now all she needed was a little more coaching and some practice. She fired at a tin can across the yard. The bullets kicked up puffs of dirt, but did not get anywhere near the can.

"You're getting the idea. Now, when you shoot, you squeeze the trigger . . ."

Across the yard, Sam was working with Tommy. He was using his father's old revolver and was enthusiastically shooting at another tin can. Though he had never worked with a gun before, he took to it naturally. Sam had only to show him a technique once for him to learn it and start to practice it.

The can was already riddled with bullet holes, and they had been working for only an hour.

"Very good," Sam said as Tommy scored another hit. "But keep in mind that anybody attacking you will not be like a tin can. He won't be standing still. And quite likely he'll be trying to kill you. That's a lot different. Don't be getting any false courage because you've had some early success."

"I understand, Sam."

"Good. Let's progress to a moving target." Sam had a stack of cans at hand. He picked up one and threw it. "Take a shot, Tommy."

The boy raised his gun and fired, missing the can by a good yard. He looked disappointed.

"What happened? I was doing so good!"

"Remember what I said about not getting too cocky? Take it a step at a time. In a situation like this, you need to kind of track the movement and anticipate where it will be by the time you shoot and the bullet arrives. Here, let me show you."

Sam picked up a can and threw it into the air. He drew his Colt and fired three times, each time sending the can zigzagging in a different direction.

"Wow!"

"Show off," Matt said.

"You made it look easy," Tommy said.

"That was the result of years of work," Sam said. "What you should have noticed was the way I directed my gun not at the can, but at where it would be . . ."

Across the yard, Lilly suddenly figured out what she

was doing wrong. She fired three times, and her can went flying through the air with three neat holes in it. She screamed in delight, hugged Matt and then ran over and picked up her son and swung him around.

"Mom!" he said, but Lilly ignored him.

"This is wonderful," Lilly said. "I can actually hit the target!"

"Doing better," Matt agreed. "Wish there was time for more practice. That's what's needed now."

"We'll do what we can," Lilly promised. "Can you show us some more?"

Sam pulled some more bullets from his bags and passed them out to the woman and boy, then watched as they carefully reloaded their weapons.

Derrell got worried when he heard the shots. He paused as he listened, trying to figure out where they were coming from. Derrell was guessing that since Matt and Sam were not in town, they were probably at Lilly's, since she seemed to be at the center of the current problems. Her place was in the general direction of where the shooting was taking place.

"I don't like the sound of that," Derrell said.

"I doubt that's anything to worry about," Lester said, stretching in the saddle to hear better. "There's only two guns, and the shots are too steady. It doesn't sound like a fight."

"Maybe. But considering how dangerous Petty is, I don't want to take any chances."

"You're right. Don't go running blindly into the situation, son. Scout it out a little before you lose your temper. Getting yourself killed won't do anybody any good. Especially the widow Brandom."

Derrell started on again at a faster pace with Lester beside him.

"I can't imagine Jack being dead," Derrell said. "We were never friends or anything, but he was always around."

"And always in your way when it came to Lilly," Lester said. "I knew you were courting her for a while. You never told me what happened."

"Not much to tell. I think the main problem was that I was out on the range a lot, looking after the cattle. Jack was closer to home, working for that little place of his. Guess Jack was more what she wanted. Or maybe he was just around more than me."

"A lot has changed in the past few years," Lester said. "Up until Petty stole the livestock, we had a pretty good operation started. We're still not broke. And if Matt helps us get our cows back, you'll be in good shape. Maybe you can be more what Lilly's looking for now."

Derrell shook his head. "It'll take her a long time to get over Jack."

"Maybe. But you've been waiting a long time for her. And there'll be a time when she starts looking around again. Trust your old man. He's seen it happen. You might consider following your heart—if that's what you want—and kind of pave the way for the future."

"I'll think about it."

"I wouldn't think too long if I were you. I wouldn't even consider trying to replace Jack. Lilly won't be able to keep this place up on her own, and if there's any spark left, you might be able to fan it into something hotter."

When Lilly's place came into view, Derrell recognized Matt, Sam, Lilly and Tommy in the front yard. Sam suddenly threw a tin can, drew his Colt, and fired several quick shots, sending the tin can zigzagging through the air.

"Looks like a little target practice," Lester said. "It's a good idea."

Derrell's heart sank a little when he saw how close Matt was standing to Lilly, helping her with the revolver. Maybe his father was right, and he'd have to start making his interest in the woman known soon. Or was he already too late?

Derrell called out, "Hello, at the house!"

The shooting stopped as the figures in the front yard turned to face them. Derrell watched Lilly closely. She took a half-step away from Matt. She smiled as she greeted the Browns. Derrell wondered if the smile was for him or was left over from Matt. He had never been very good around women and wasn't sure what to think.

"Come on in!" Lilly said. "Matt and Sam are helping us learn how to protect ourselves a little better."

"Couldn't hurt," Derrell agreed. "I'd hate to see either of you two hurt."

"Watch this!" Tommy said, and peppered an already battered tin can with bullets. It bounced in the dirt as if it were alive.

Lester chuckled. "I think the boy's a natural!"

"Don't fill his head with ideas," Lilly warned, though her face showed she was actually proud of her son.

* * *

Marshal Holt, Hardesty, and Cooper also heard the shooting in the distance. Holt stopped his horse and acted as if he were going to turn back to town.

"There's been too many bullets flying to suit me," Holt said. "Maybe we'll make this visit another time."

Cooper moved his horse to block the path.

"I don't think so," he said. "King wanted us to make this visit. We've already been on the receiving end of his craziness. I don't intend to give him any other opportunities."

Hardesty rubbed the sore spots on his body and groaned slightly. "Maybe you'd like to be the one to tell King we failed again. Not me."

"I suppose not." A few minutes later the Brandom homestead could be seen, and Holt moaned slightly at all the figures in the front yard. "Damn! They have an army down there! And Two-Wolves is among them. How could I ride into that bunch . . . it would be suicide."

"Going back to King and telling him you failed might be slow torture and suicide," Cooper reminded the marshal.

"Don't worry," Hardesty said. "Here's the plan. Holt, you go on down there with your official badge and your official shovel and inform them the law requires their cooperation. Cooper and I will position ourselves so that when Two-Wolves and the others come up to stop you, we can open fire on them. This time we'll succeed. It shouldn't take more than a few well-placed bullets to even things up with those two."

"One thing wrong with that plan," Holt protested.

"I'll be out there in the open like a sitting duck. I'll be the one risking my neck while you guys are up here, nice and hidden and out of the line of fire."

Cooper shrugged. "One of the hazards of your job."

"I still don't like it."

"So who asked you?" Hardesty pointed to the grave on the hill. "That's where Brandom is buried. You go on down and we'll get ourselves ready."

Holt hitched up his pants as best he could while still sitting in the saddle and started down the hill toward the house.

Sam reloaded his gun and glanced up at the Browns. "What brings you out this way?"

"Wish we could say it was to cook up another batch of fish," Lester joked. "But none of us have had much spare time recently!"

Sam laughed. "You could say that again!"

Derrell stepped down from his horse, approached Matt, and said, "Actually, we're here representing the town of Snake Creek. Maybe you didn't know it, but Charlie and Henry are members of the town council. They called a special meeting this morning."

"I don't think I like the sound of this," Matt said.

"Just hear the man out," Sam suggested.

"Anyway, the council decided to ask you to take the job of marshal," Derrell continued. "Holt will be fired as soon as you say you'll do it."

"Sorry. Not interested."

"Why not? We all need you. You've already indicated you'll help in the fight against Petty. This will just give you the power of the law."

"I've served as a Texas Ranger, along with a lot of other jobs. But to be honest, I don't like working for others. The minute you accept somebody else's money, you have to start following their way of doing things. I don't like being penned in that way."

"They told me that you would have free rein to do whatever you felt needed to be done. Nobody would interfere with you."

"I won't back away from the fight. But I'll not accept your offer. You can tell the council thanks, but no thanks."

"Charlie even said that if you take the job, you can have unlimited meals at his place . . . on the house!"

Sam laughed and said, "By golly, they must be desperate, to make that offer after seeing the way he put the food away yesterday!"

"If I were convinced I would be more help as marshal than as a private citizen, I would take the job," Matt said. "Especially considering Charlie's generous offer! But I just don't feel comfortable with it at this time."

Derrell shook his head. "Well, at least we tried." He turned to Lilly. "Are you getting pretty good at this shooting, too?"

"Better than I expected."

Derrell pulled his rifle. "How about if I show you a few tricks, as well?"

"That'd be just fine!" Lilly said.

Derrell approached the woman and placed her hands in the proper position. Matt noticed that Lilly gave Derrell a smile that had a sparkle in it that was missing when he had been helping her. He grinned at Sam and stepped out of the way.

"A better man than you?" Sam joked in a soft voice.

"A different kind of man. I wasn't making a play for her, anyway. She wasn't my type."

"Right. She has a little too much class!"

Matt pretended to punch Sam on the shoulder, but stopped when he saw Marshal Holt come into sight near Jack's grave on the hill.

"This is becoming a popular place," Matt said. "Looks like we have another visitor."

Chapter 13

"I know I don't like this," Matt said, watching Holt ride over the hill near Jack Brandom's grave.

"Holt by himself isn't a big problem," Sam said, "but if he's here, some of King's other men probably aren't too far behind."

"Lilly doesn't need this."

"Can't say I'm real enthused about it, myself."

Matt looked over at Derrell and Lilly, who were still working with the rifle and talking among themselves. "We've got more company," Matt said. "We're going up to check it out."

Derrell took his rifle back from Lilly. "Remember what I showed you. I'm going with Matt and Sam. Dad will stay here with you and Tommy."

Lester nodded.

"Be on your guard," Sam warned as Derrell fell into step beside the two blood brothers and walked up the hill.

Holt had taken a shovel from his saddle and placed its tip in the still-soft dirt of the grave. He hadn't actually started to dig when Matt, Sam, and Derrell arrived.

"What's going on here?" Matt demanded.

"You boys just stay calm," Holt said, looking distinctly uncomfortable. "I'm just doing my duty."

"You're scum," Derrell said.

Sam and Matt stared at Holt. The marshal seemed to wilt under their gazes.

"Look," he said. "I'm just doing my job. A citizen in town has been accused of a crime. He pleads innocent. The only evidence we have is the body. It's within my jurisdiction to gather all the evidence I need."

Holt pushed the tip of the shovel into the dirt. Matt grabbed the handle in an iron grip. Holt could not budge the shovel, though a light sweat broke out on his forehead. Sam took Holt's arm and forced his hand from the handle.

"There are different ways of looking at this, I suppose," Sam said. "I'm not a lawyer, but a case could be made that a marshal does have certain powers. Even if it does seem to some as if he is harassing an innocent widow woman."

"And we could beat the crap out of this person, though that would also be illegal," Matt continued. "Even though he may be a sorry excuse for a man, he does wear a badge."

"So what alternatives does that leave us?"

Holt looked at them both as if they were crazy. His eyes glanced from one to the other, trying to follow the talk.

"We could go ahead and try to beat some sense into this fellow, which might be morally right but legally wrong," Matt said.

"On the other hand, if there was a person in office with a stronger moral character, there would be no need to beat him . . . except for the fun of it. I imagine some legal basis could be found if we looked hard enough."

"You've convinced me." Matt turned to Derrell. "I've been thinking about our talk a little earlier, and I've reconsidered my position. I'll be glad to accept the job as City Marshal."

Holt's mouth flew open in surprise. Of all the possible things that could have happened, this was not one he'd thought of.

"You can't do that!" Holt said. "The council has to vote on it! King will eat all of them and spit them out for breakfast. There's no way any of them would go against King Petty! You're all lying!"

Derrell smiled broadly. "Well, that's more like it. I don't know what's the proper way of swearing you in, but I think since the council said you have the job immediately upon acceptance, you're now the new marshal."

"Sounds good," Matt said. "We'll take care of the paperwork later."

A heavy sweat was now pouring down Holt's face. He stood as if rooted to the spot, not knowing what to do next.

"We do need to attend to one thing," Sam said, gesturing to his chest.

"Of course!" Matt reached out and plucked the badge from Holt's shirt, polished it on his sleeve, and pinned it to his own chest. "Now. Guess that makes it legal enough."

"What is your first act as marshal?" Sam asked.

"To order this trespasser off the Brandom land," Matt answered. "Get out, Holt, or else—"

A rifle shot exploded from some brush on the other side of the hill.

"Here we go again," Sam said.

Lilly had to admit to herself that even though she had never before liked guns, she did like the feeling she had when she handled the guns well and hit her intended target. Matt had gotten her started, and Derrell had continued with her.

Was it only the night before that Holt and Conn had paid her that visit? She had been so frightened for the safety of her and Tommy that she could barely function. Now, though only a few hours later, she felt things had changed. It was not just that Sam, Matt, and Derrell were present, but that she was doing something on her own to help herself and not depending entirely on somebody else.

Lilly could see her friends talking with Holt on the hill. She thought back several years and tried to remember why she had rejected Derrell's advances in favor of Jack. Both were good men, and always had been. For some reason, years before, Jack just seemed to be the best choice. And he had provided her a good life for as long as it lasted. She had not regretted marrying Jack. She still thought of Derrell from time to time, though they seldom talked. She was a little surprised to see Derrell again . . . unless he was still interested in her. He had never married, after all. It was too soon to even think of such things, but maybe in a year. . . .

She jumped when the rifle shot exploded from some brush near the hill, followed by another shot on the other side of the hill. Somebody was obviously trying to pin down her friends, who had already scurried for cover.

"Best get inside, ma'am," Lester said. "You, too, Tommy."

"But they're shooting!" Tommy protested.

"That's why you'd best get inside. There's not much you can do here. No use taking chances."

"What are you planning to do?"

"Go up and help my son, of course. If you all get inside where it's safe."

"We'll do it."

"Good."

Lester started up the hill, staying close to the trees and brush.

Sam went in one direction and Matt the other. They blended into the underbrush so well that they could not even be noticed, and the shooting stopped almost as quickly as it had started.

Holt attempted to sneak away. He was stopped when Derrell reached out and grabbed him by his shirt.

"Not so fast," Derrell said. "Where do you think you're going?"

"Bodine ordered me to get out," Holt answered. "I'm just trying to oblige . . ."

Matt crawled back to where Derrell had pinned Holt. "I've changed my mind. You're staying here awhile. You were setting us up. Who's with you?"

"Hardesty. Cooper. That's all."

"Petty's not with them?"

"Not this time."

Holt suddenly twisted and scampered away. Derrell stood to go after him. Matt said, "Don't worry about him. If he's smart, he'll get out of the area for good . . . before Petty gets hold of him. Right now, I'm more concerned about the other two."

Higher on the hill, Sam was working his way around the spot from which one of the shots had come. He moved quickly but silently until he was looking down at a familiar face topped with red hair.

"Haven't we met before?" Sam asked.

Hardesty looked up in amazement as Sam dropped and slid down the hill. He raised his rifle to shoot, but was not fast enough. Sam lifted his Colt and fired without hesitation. The bullet ripped through flesh and into the heart, killing the outlaw instantly.

Even as he fell, Sam started around to the other side of the hill.

Cooper knew they had failed again as soon as they missed with the first shots. With men like Bodine and Two-Wolves, you didn't get a second chance. Cooper heard the single shot from the other side of the hill, knew that Hardesty had bought the farm, and that it would be his turn next.

The outlaw looked around, searching for an escape route, and knew there was none. The only path was downhill, toward the house. On the other hand, the woman and boy were there. He thought maybe he could take one of them as a hostage and bargain his way to safety.

It was his only chance.

Cooper crawled down the hill, keeping hidden in the brush as much as possible. He made good progress, motivated by desperation, until he was almost to the house.

"Got you covered. Come on out."

It was an unfamiliar voice. Cooper jumped to his feet and started to run. Behind him, an older man with bushy eyebrows took a shot at him but missed. Cooper ran as quickly as he could, until he got to the house. He didn't pause, but kicked the door open and forced his way inside.

Only to look into the barrels of two guns staring him in the face. Lilly was holding a rifle, and the boy was holding a small hand gun. At close range, both would be deadly.

The thug started to back up to the door, even as he raised his gun toward the mother and son.

Both fired at the same time. The bullets hit with such an impact that they propelled Cooper backward through the door into the yard. Matt and Derrell were standing next to the door, ready to go in after the thug. They aimed their guns at the figure flying past, but could tell at a glance that their help wasn't needed this time.

Cooper hit the ground hard, bounced twice, and then lay still.

Matt walked up to the body as the mother and son came through the door. Lilly was almost shaking. Tommy's face was expressionless.

"Good shooting," Matt said. "Don't think they expected you to be prepared for them this time."

"I . . . killed him . . . ," Lilly said. "I've never even shot a gun before today, and now I've killed a man . . ."

Derrell reached out to Lilly, allowing her to bury her face in his chest as she sobbed.

"You had no choice," Derrell said. "You've got to protect yourself. You did the right thing."

Sam walked down the hill and said, "Derrell's right. It's not easy shooting a man. But remember how you felt last night . . . how helpless you felt. Now you know at least you're not helpless. Keep that in mind."

Tommy stepped forward, and Derrell put his arm around him as well.

Matt and Sam stepped to one side as Derrell talked with Lilly and the boy. Lester joined them.

"Your son's good with them," Sam observed.

"Yes, he is," Lester said proudly. He gestured to Matt's chest. "Looks like he talked you into taking the job, after all?"

"There was a good argument for my doing so," Matt explained. "So I changed my mind."

"What's the next step?"

"Bring the fight to Petty. Let's go get your cattle."

Chapter 14

"No. Absolutely not." Lilly's voice was firm. "Tommy is not going to go with you."

The others in the room—Henry and Clarissa Ponder, Derrell and Lester Brown, Matt and Sam—looked at her in surprise. She had apparently changed a lot in the past few days. She was more forceful, more strong-willed.

"He's your kid," Sam said. "Nobody has the right to tell you what to do. But he wants to go."

"Please, Mom!" Tommy said. "It'll be good for me."

"This isn't some kind of picnic," Lilly said sternly. "Matt and Sam are going into dangerous territory. They could get killed. You could get killed. This isn't something you're doing for fun."

"I handled myself back at home," Tommy protested.

"They also weren't looking for us to have guns and know how to use them."

"But I know how to use a gun now. I want to do something that'll make a difference. I want to help."

"You can help by staying here and staying safe. I don't want you to start down that road."

"What road?"

"Where you feel you aren't a man unless you have a gun in your hand . . . where you are constantly in a fight . . . where you are never sure if you'll be living through the day . . ."

"But I want to be able to face what I have to face . . . I never want to be caught helpless . . ."

Clarissa spoke up. "We could go on like this forever. Like Sam said, nobody can tell you what to do with your kid. But there's lots of people who've done a man's job at his age. And you might consider respecting his wishes."

"It might help the boy," Derrell said softly. "He needs to find his own way. And, let's face it, there won't be many times that he'll have as many of us looking out for him as there are today!"

"And I want to go!"

Lilly sighed. "Looks like I'm outnumbered. But I still don't like it."

Matt patted Tommy on the back and said, "Good to have you with us."

Sam grinned. "We could use one of Petty's and Holt's arguments. An allegation has been made, and Matt as marshal is simply investigating and returning stolen property to its rightful owners. Not that anybody would question us too much."

"They'd be too busy shooting!" Matt laughed. Then he looked at Lilly. "Just joking, of course. It won't be that dangerous."

"Don't humor me, Matt. I said I'd let him go. You lie to me and I might change my mind."

Matt decided to pursue a safer line of discussion. "Hmm . . . let's talk strategy. Lester, Derrell, you two know this area better than anybody else. What do you think's going on with the stolen cattle?"

"They're being herded and penned up somewhere, until they can get them to market up north," Lester said. "There's no doubt of that. Only problem is that I haven't figured out where that is. Not yet. And I haven't had the guts or the manpower to look into it further."

"It's probably in some of those hills up north," Derrell added. "There's some hollows and hills up there that might serve that purpose."

"It doesn't take a genius to track a herd of cows," Matt said. "I tracked your rustlers a little ways, before that ill-fated fish fry. It shouldn't be that hard to find them. Even if we have some problems, Sam will be able to figure it out. He's the best tracker I know, and I've known some good ones."

"True enough," Lester added. "The main problem is not finding the cows, but in keeping Petty from finding us. Matt, you and Sam have evened things up a lot, but last I looked, he still has more guns than we have. And I know he's got at least some men with the cattle. It won't be a cake walk. I have to agree with Lilly about that."

"So we'll have to leave separately so as not to raise suspicion on Petty's part," Matt said. "Find the cattle. And move fast—real fast—so that we can get back before Petty knows what hit him. And before he has a chance to try any more tricks with Lilly."

"That means we don't delay a minute," Sam explained. "We need to act this morning. Within the hour. We have a slight advantage in that Holt has disappeared from sight. So while Petty knows that his men failed—I imagine he expected them to—he doesn't know that the city council is also opposing him. That will probably come out real soon, and there's no telling how he'll react. So we haven't a minute to lose."

"Lilly, you need to stay with Clarissa and Henry until we get back. It's best that nobody knows where you are or where to find you. The homestead can get by a day or so without you. Clarissa and Henry already said you're welcome here."

"I just don't understand any of this," Lilly said. "I don't like any of this."

"Chances are nobody ever will," Matt said. "All we can do is the best we can. And for now, that means fighting Petty in every way we can. We will win against him. There is no doubt of that. The problem is how to keep you and Tommy safe in the meantime."

"Would you let me see that gun?" Sam asked. Lilly handed him the revolver. Sam broke it open, checked its action, then placed it and some additional bullets on the table. "Be sure to remember what we showed you. Keep this with you at all times."

Lilly sighed again. "I'll do what you say. I still don't like it."

"None of us do, Lilly. None of us do."

Lilly had no expression on her face as the others left the room at different times to meet at the agreed-upon spot. Tommy and Derrell were the last ones to leave.

"I guess it's tough to let go," Clarissa said.

"Yes. More than I thought. It's happening a lot sooner than I planned."

"I don't have any kids, so I can only guess. But I know it's tough to let somebody go that you love. Husband or son."

Clarissa turned slowly and sat down at the table near Lilly.

"It hurts so much," Lilly said without looking at the other woman. "Jack being gone, I mean. Everybody's been so nice, and I'm trying to be strong, as if it's no problem. I smile, make biscuits, and sometimes for a minute or two at a time I feel almost like it'll be all right. But I can never really get it out of my mind."

Clarissa patted Lilly on the arm.

"What you're feeling is just natural," Clarissa said. "It's only been a few days. In time the hurt will fade away. You will continue with your life. Who knows? You might even grow and become a better person."

"I already find myself doing things differently than when Jack was alive. It's kind of scary."

"Do you like it?"

"Yes. That's what's scary. It's not me."

Clarissa grinned. "I don't see anybody else but you here."

"You know what I mean!"

"Yes. I do. Nobody is going to say your husband getting killed was a good thing. But you still have your life. You owe it to yourself and to your son to do the best you can for yourself. If that means change . . . then why fight it?"

"And Tommy?"

"He'll also change a lot. But that's not bad. Sometimes we have to say goodbye so that we can find a new life, even if we are not unhappy with the old life. Just give it some time."

Lilly sighed. "You're a very smart woman, Clarissa. Wish I had some of what you have."

"You have more than you realize. A lot of people wouldn't have been able to face what you've had to deal with over the past few days. Don't sell yourself short."

"I'll try to remember that. Do you have any more advice?"

"Yes. As a matter of fact, I do."

"Please. Tell me."

Clarissa picked up the gun from the table, reached over, and slipped it into Lilly's apron pocket.

"Keep the gun handy."

Ralph Smiley stopped by the little campfire where the coffeepot was always boiling. The coffee was so thick and strong that he could almost cut it with a knife, but it helped to cut the dust from his throat. With the new cattle taken from the Browns, Smiley almost had enough to make another trip north. He normally might have had enough anyway, but the newest additions were such good examples of beef flesh that he had gotten to thinking about alternate plans. He had always wanted his own ranch, but his life had never let him stay in one place long enough. Maybe it was time to change the situation.

Even in a short drive several head were generally lost in any case. Maybe he could "lose" a few of the Brown cattle along the way—that he could come back to later. There was a bull that the Browns owned that would be a good match for the cattle, and it would be enough to give him a start.

It was a bold plan for Smiley, considering that he was working for a man who seemed to enjoy killing as much as drinking and eating. The only problem would be Ash Crawford. The other men probably couldn't care less about the loss of a few head, but Crawford seemed to dog Smiley's every move and threaten retaliation for a single misstep. He seemed to enjoy intimidation almost as much as King Petty.

Somehow it just didn't seem fair.

Ash rode by, smiled an evil-looking grin, waved, and continued on.

On the other hand, this wasn't such a bad life. It was the best job he ever had. Maybe it was better not to rock the boat, after all. If he could keep from crossing Petty, he could continue to live the good life. After all, what could go wrong other than a storm, stampede, or other hazard inherent to the life of a cowboy?

Smiley threw the dregs of the bitter coffee to the ground and went back to his job.

Matt took the lead. He was not as good at tracking as Sam, but it didn't take a Cheyenne scout to follow the trail, even though it was a few days old.

"Up through here." Matt gestured to some steep hills just ahead of the group. "That's where they're headed. Three men and a bunch of cattle."

Lester Brown pushed back his hat and scratched his bushy gray hair.

"Are you sure of that, Matt?"

"Positive. Why?"

"I've rode this land for quite a few years, and don't remember anyplace up there that would hold that many cattle."

"That's where the tracks lead. Guess there's only one way to find out."

"Lead on."

The group went slowly, carefully watching for any guards that might have been posted along the way. So far, they had seen none. It had been a clear trail with nobody trying to stop them. Matt figured that Petty and his men were so confident that they didn't even consider the possibility of anybody crossing them.

These hills were just a short distance outside of town and seemed to rise from the relatively flat land near the creek. Matt halted suddenly and stopped the group, gesturing for them to move off the main trail. Sam took off from the group to scout ahead.

"There it is," Matt said. "Looks like a good-sized hollow down there."

"And an entrance big enough for some livestock to pass through, but hidden from view otherwise," Lester said. "How do you like that?"

It was difficult to see much on the other side of the entry, though Matt could see the brown backs of a few cows wandering around.

Sam returned in just a few minutes.

"It's a large area, surrounded by steep hills on three sides," he reported. "The only way in is through the main opening, down there, or along the ledges over-head. Matt, you and I have climbed a lot worse places. I can't speak for the rest of you."

"How do you feel about it, son?" Derrell asked Tommy. "I doubt if you've had much climbing experience on your homestead. You can stay here and watch the horses."

Tommy gritted his teeth and said, "I want to go."

Sam tied his horse deep in the brush where it could not be seen by anybody passing on the trail. "This way," he said. "Let's split up and meet on the other side. Tommy, you can go with Derrell. I don't think they'll be able to see us, but be careful, anyway. No use taking chances."

Maybe to Matt and Sam it was no great deal, but to a ten-year-old boy who had never climbed before, the trip into the valley was a scary feat.

Tommy climbed quickly at first, keeping pace with Derrell, who seemed to move up the hill as if it were nothing out of the ordinary. The higher Tommy climbed, the steeper the hill got, and the boy found himself clutching at roots and branches to keep his balance.

"Here's where the fun really starts," Derrell said. He was waiting for Tommy to catch up. Just on the other side of some bushes was a narrow dirt ledge that bordered a hundred-foot drop-off. Though it was only thirty feet long, it looked like a mile. And, worse, for that thirty feet they would be exposed to anybody glancing up from below.

"This is the only way in?" Tommy asked.

"It is for us. The paths the others are taking are even more difficult. You sure you want to try it?"

"I'm not going to chicken out now."

"Good for you. Just follow my lead. Stay close to

the hill. And don't look down. It'll go faster than you might think."

"Especially if we go down?"

Derrell grinned. "I'm glad you can joke about it. Just stay calm. You'll do fine."

Derrell stepped out on the ledge. He kept his feet wide apart and his hands on the hillside. Tommy noted that the ledge was wider than it first appeared—almost two feet at its widest spot. Derrell moved slowly but steadily, taking one small step at a time in smooth, sliding motions.

In a minute, he was a third of the way across.

"Come on," Derrell whispered. "You can do it."

Tommy breathed deeply and took the first step.

The breath seemed to catch in his throat, and he felt an emptiness in the pit of his stomach. He had a strong urge to dig his fingers into the hill and never let go. Instead, he took a very small step in the same way that he had seen Derrell do.

"Good," Derrell said. "You've got it started. Just come on."

Tommy took another step, and then another. Gradually, he started to breathe more normally.

"How am I doing?" he asked, surprised at how normal his voice sounded.

"Great! Watch out for the next step. There's some loose dirt and rocks there. Check your footing before you go any farther."

Tommy glanced down at the ledge, and for an instant caught a glimpse of empty space just a few inches away from his heels. He closed his eyes, shut them tightly, then started again. The dirt was a little slippery for the next few steps, but Tommy held more tightly to the hill and worked his way through the rocks. At one point he accidentally kicked off a loose stone. He froze, expecting a bullet to hit him in the back from below. When no shot came, he continued on.

To his surprise, Derrell was already on the other side of the ledge waiting for him.

"Two more steps, son. You can do it."

Tommy almost leaped to safety beside Derrell. They ducked into the brush, in case the rock that Tommy knocked loose had brought them any unwanted attention. Below them, however, were only cattle. If any of the rustlers had heard the stone falling, they hadn't paid it any attention.

Tommy rubbed his sweaty forehead with the back of his hand.

"That had to be the longest walk I've ever had," he said.

"And it took all of three minutes," Derrell said. "Told you it wouldn't be long, once you get into it."

Tommy felt as proud as he ever had. His dad had praised him for building a good fence or doing a good job plowing the field. This achievement seemed different, more exciting, and he felt pleased at his accomplishment and at Derrell's praise.

"You did good," he said. "Now let's find Matt and the others and see what we do next."

Chapter 15

All of the small group—Matt, Sam, Lester and Derrell Brown, and Tommy—had made it safely into the valley. They had a clear view of the valley from where they were hidden behind the rock outcropping. Below them, the cattle moved slowly, munching on grass, while the rustlers watched over them.

"This is a pretty place," Derrell said. "Lucky for us that Sam found that entrance. I've been here all my life, and didn't know about this valley. Even though that entrance is big enough for cattle to get through, it was sure hard to spot."

"And that climb was the scenic route for sure." Matt laughed. "But we're here now, and that's the main thing."

"My daddy would never have let me make that climb," Tommy said.

Derrell put his hand on the boy's shoulder and said, "It was a dangerous climb. You could have been killed. Your daddy would have looked out for you the best way he knew how."

"Yeah. I know. Sam told me something like that already."

"Sam was right. Your daddy was a good man. Now it's your turn to do him proud. Just like you're doing for all of us."

Matt looked at Sam, and they both smiled. The more they knew Derrell Brown, the better they liked him. He may not have been the best fighter or the smartest man the blood brothers had ever met, but he had a good heart and was proving himself to be a solid, dependable man. He was also quickly making a place in the hearts of Lilly and Tommy.

"So what's the plan now?" Lester asked.

"I've been thinking about that," Matt answered. "Seems to me like we need to accomplish two things. One is to get your cattle back. Along with the other ranchers' in the area. The second thing is to beat King Petty at his own game. Look down there, and what do you see?"

Smiley and his men were riding leisurely around the cattle, looking them over. The cattle were munching on grass or drinking from the stream. In the distance was the entrance to the valley between the rock outcroppings that was hidden from the outside.

"I see some cattle. A few men. What else is there?"

"I see only one way out of the valley. I see nobody guarding it, and the men down there for the most part are not gunfighters. The question is how to get the cattle with, hopefully, no bloodshed. I'd suggest a little stampede through the entrance."

"Hmm. Could work. Don't think they have enough men down there to turn a stampede. Especially if it catches them by surprise."

"After they get back in the open, you can always cut out yours. Word will get to the others. And just let Petty try something. We'll be waiting."

The others nodded in agreement.

"My dad and I will go down and work with the cattle," Derrell said. "I'd say we know cattle about as well as anybody here."

"I want to go with Derrell," Tommy said.

"No, it'd be too dangerous. Cattle can be pretty tricky sometimes. You need to learn a little more before you risk getting caught in the middle of a herd of crazed cows."

"Sam's probably our best shot," Matt continued. "He can stay up here and over us, in case something goes wrong. Tommy, you'd be safest up here with him."

"I'd rather be with Derrell . . ."

"Tommy," Derrell said. "You need to listen to Matt. He makes sense."

"All right. I'll stay with Sam."

"I'll go down with the Browns. If necessary, I can help take out the outlaws guarding the pass. We need to keep ourselves hidden, though, until we're ready to make our move. It will mean another climb down."

Derrell looked down at the gradual slope and laughed softly.

"Compared to the trip in, this will be a piece of cake," he said.

"Hell, this should be a lot of fun," Lester said. "I've been waiting a long time to get back at King Petty."

"Once we're down there, it should be easy to get the action going," Derrell continued. "There's one old gal in that bunch that kind of likes to take the lead, but she's spooky as the dickens. Once she goes, the others will follow."

"Then let's get to it. The party's waiting!"

Lilly looked around the empty room. Clarissa was in the front of the store with her husband, leaving her to herself and her thoughts. With Tommy gone, it seemed even more lonely than before. Lilly wasn't sure why she had let the boy go with Sam, Matt, and the others. He was just a boy. It was dangerous. So why had she let him?

He had wanted to go.

That was a silly reason. And it wasn't really a good reason, considering that he might be killed, just as Jack had been.

Lilly touched the door frame and looked out at Henry and Clarissa, talking quietly between themselves as they worked in the store. She quietly envied them their marriage and their life. She'd had a good life with Jack, but now Jack was gone. As Clarissa said, Lilly still had her life in front of her. What would that bring? She wasn't sure what she wanted anymore. She wasn't sure she wanted to get married again, though it would be almost impossible for her to work the farm by herself, and Tommy needed a father.

Outside the front store window, the sun was shining brightly. Spring was now in full bloom. The flowers in the front yard of her home had exploded in full color, and though she had been away only a few hours, she already missed them. She thought of Derrell Brown, and how she had once cared for him, and how he had been so kind to her. Since Jack's death, she had been

blessed with many persons helping her. Henry and
Clarissa Ponder. Sam and Matt. Derrell Brown. But
Derrell had been the most solid, the most dependable.
Of all her friends, Derrell had made her feel the most
secure and the most wanted.

It was an unexpected feeling.

Lilly missed her husband. Nobody could ever replace him. It would take a long time to get over the
hurt. At the same time, as Clarissa had pointed out,
Lilly was changing, and the changes were not all bad.

The gun in her apron pocket was one example.

When Jack was alive, she had never felt afraid. Lilly
had always let him take care of things. She had never
felt the need to do more than take care of the house
and her son. When Jack was alive, the thought of
learning how to shoot, much less carrying a loaded
revolver, would never have crossed her mind.

Then, suddenly, Jack was gone and the world was a
horrible place, full of terrors. She had to learn how to
take care of herself, and quickly. She could no longer
depend on somebody else to take care of her.

The street outside the window seemed deserted.
None of King Petty's men had threatened her since she
had helped to kill the outlaw the day before. She knew,
however, that the danger was not past. Thanks to
Matt's and Derrell's lessons in marksmanship she was
better prepared than she had ever been before. She was
learning to stand on her own.

And that is also why she let Tommy go with the
others. Jack would never have allowed it. Tommy
would have grown up with the same false sense of
security that Lilly had. Though only a kid, this was a

chance for Tommy to do something on his own. Lilly
felt she could not deny him that.

Lilly thought again about her husband, and almost
felt his presence near her.

"Jack, I know Tommy and I are doing lots of things
you wouldn't approve of," she said softly, closing her
eyes and remembering the way he used to stand with
his arms around her as they looked out from the porch
at their farm. "But things are different now. And
there'll be lots more changes. You did your best. You
were a good man and I loved you. But I'm changing.
Tommy's changing. There'll come a time when I will
move on. I may even get married again. I hope you
understand that. We used to talk about that, and we
agreed that would be the best thing. Of course, we
laughed. We never thought that day would come. I
wish it would have been different."

She sat back down at the table and placed her head
in her hands.

"Jack, I know if you were alive you'd try to put a
stop to all this. You'd say the best way to avoid trouble is to walk around it. But Petty brought the trouble
to you, and to your family. It couldn't be avoided.
Now we're bringing the fight back to him, with the
help of some friends you never had the chance to
know. There's no stopping it now. I don't know where
it will end. All I know is that we're in it until the end.
I'm sorry it had to be this way. I really am."

The sound of a creaking door interrupted Lilly's
thoughts. She raised her head and opened her eyes and
saw Clarissa looking at her thoughtfully.

"Are you all right?" Clarissa asked.

"I think I will be now," Lilly said. "Like you said, it'll just take some time."

Smiley rode leisurely through the cattle, but something felt wrong. It was not something he could put his finger on. It was more like the vague feeling he got before a storm hit even though the sky remained clear. The fact that Ash Crawford watched his every move didn't help.

Ash rode his large horse toward Smiley. The cattle moved restlessly out of his way. Smiley let the other man catch up to him.

"Just got back from town," Ash said. "The picture there ain't too pretty."

"What's going on?"

"While we've been out here with these damned cows, King's been having himself some problems. A couple of strangers are in town, causing him some trouble."

"How come he hasn't dealt with them like he has everybody else?"

Ash leaned forward, putting his hands on the saddle horn.

"I think these two have even King worried. They've been making chopped meat out of his guys. They even killed Hardesty and Cooper. And Holt's disappeared from sight."

"You get any names?"

"A couple of yahoos named Bodine and Two-Wolves."

Smiley stood straight up in the saddle, suddenly

very nervous as he realized the storm that he had been worried about.

"Did you say Bodine? Matt Bodine? And Sam Two-Wolves?"

"Yeah." Ash's eyes narrowed in suspicion. "How'd you know that?"

Smiley nudged his horse forward, to continue his circle around the cattle. He scanned the countryside, trying to spot anything out of the ordinary, but knew that if Bodine or Two-Wolves were in the area, chances of spotting them would be slim.

"I know about them," Smiley said. "I worked some range up north for a while, where they run some cattle. I was younger then, and more foolish. Those two had some good beeves, and some of us thought about moving in on it. A couple of my buddies got a little too enthusiastic and tried it without me."

"Trying to cut you out?" Ash laughed.

"Right. Good thing for me they did. Bodine and Two-Wolves caught them in the act. My buddies didn't have a chance. They tried to shoot their way out and were dead before they knew what hit them. I skipped out of that country, and haven't been back since."

"Bad hombres, eh?"

"If I were Petty, I'd be real concerned."

Ash loosened the gun in his holster and moved closer to Smiley.

"And if I were you, I wouldn't get any ideas about skipping out on King and me. I've seen you work. I know you're probably trying to think of a way out even now. Don't try it. You still know cattle better than anybody else, and you're going to stick around to the end. Got it?"

"With Bodine and Two-Wolves, the end might come a lot sooner than any of us expect."

Ash spit and directed his horse away from the cattle.

"Maybe. I'm going to take a look around. If those two are anywhere near here, we'll see how tough they are."

Matt was the leader of the group, which planned to steal back the cattle that had been previously stolen from the ranchers and farmers in the area around Snake Creek. He smiled as he crawled on his belly down the hill, finding it humorous that he was involved in this semilegal act after he had agreed to serve as marshal.

His early training with Sam's father now came in handy, as his movement barely made a ripple in the grass even though he was in one of the more open spots on the hill. He knew the others were working their way down by a less direct route, which would give them less chance of being seen. He glanced above him, to where Sam was watching. Matt wasn't sure he liked having the boy along. Something could always go wrong and the boy could be hurt. On the other hand, as crazy as Petty was, the boy was probably as safe with Sam as he would have been anywhere.

Matt continued several more feet, then rose behind one of the cattle. He stood in a crouch, hidden from view of any of the riders. They were situated well, with the valley entrance in front of the herd. Matt could see a sliver of Derrell Brown's shirt in a similar position as he looked for the nervous old gal he had mentioned. It probably wouldn't take much to stampede the critters in any case, but Matt was willing to let Derrell do it his way.

The steer in front of Matt started to walk nervously. Matt moved slowly, trying to remain hidden, when something else rippled the grass in front of the animal. Matt knew it was another snake. The steer, startled, seemed to jump straight up and sideways, leaving Matt exposed for a second.

Matt fell to the ground to hide in the grass, but he didn't move fast enough.

Not a hundred yards away, Ralph Smiley looked at him in disbelief as he clutched at his gun.

Chapter 16

Smiley felt like he had seen a ghost. Maybe it was his imagination. He had just been talking about Matt Bodine, and almost immediately Smiley had seen Bodine's face, only to immediately disappear. The rustler, however, felt a sinking feeling in his stomach. He fumbled for his gun, pulled it, then quietly put it back into the holster. There was no need to panic. Not when Bodine could outdraw him so easily.

Bodine was there. That would mean Two-Wolves would also be present. That meant trouble . . . big trouble.

The movement of the steer was what had caught his eye. Apparently the animal had been startled by one of the snakes that were so common to this area. If the steer hadn't been scared, Smiley would never have seen Bodine.

Crawford was right about one thing. He wanted to get away, and would if he could. But Ash was still watching him, so escape was impossible. He also didn't want to sound the alarm, not yet. Maybe it was only his overactive imagination.

Smiley stealthily loosened the gun in his holster without drawing attention to himself and walked his horse carefully around the steers to the place where he thought he might have seen Bodine.

Nothing.

If Bodine had been there, he had disappeared as if he had been a ghost.

So it could have been Bodine. He was almost an Indian in his ability to blend into the countryside. If it had been Bodine, he would not have stayed around for Smiley just to walk up and say hello.

Smiley felt a prickling at the back of his neck. He was being watched. The rustler looked around, but could see nobody. Not even Ash was in sight.

The cattle were meandering around restlessly. Smiley pushed his horse through the animals, trying to find something out of place, to at least catch a glimpse of Bodine or Two-Wolves. What were they planning?

Ash had dropped from sight. Smiley looked toward the valley opening. Maybe he could get away. Chances were not good. There were many steers between him and the opening, and there was an open space where Ash could easily shoot him in the back. At least Bodine wouldn't shoot him in the back. He might have a better chance with Bodine.

The cattle seemed to be getting more restless, as if they were also anticipating some kind of trouble. Smiley stood in his stirrups and stretched, looking all around the area. On the other side of the herd were two of his men, riding along as if they didn't suspect a thing.

And then Smiley saw the movement. It was in some

brush a hundred yards from where he was riding, just outside of the circle of cattle.

Smiley pulled his gun again and rode toward the brush.

"What am I looking for, Sam?"

"The main thing, Tommy, is to keep track of the enemy. You can get a good view of them from up here. Notice those two over there. They don't suspect anything. Their eyes are only on the cattle. But that one down below? He's suspicious. I don't think he's spotted any of our guys. He's just careful."

Tommy raised his gun. Instantly Sam reached out and pushed the gun back down, hoping the sun hadn't reflected off it.

"What's the matter, Sam?"

"In a situation like this, you need to be very careful. You brought your gun up before it was necessary. Sunlight could hit it and reveal your presence."

"I'm . . . sorry."

"You couldn't have known. Now you do. I know it won't happen again." Sam looked warily down into the valley. "I don't think any harm's been done."

Tommy tapped Sam's arm lightly. "Down below. There's another of the rustlers. And there's Matt. Behind that steer. I almost didn't notice him."

"That's the idea," Sam said. The steer jumped unexpectedly, exposing Matt briefly before he again disappeared into the brush. "The ideal is not to be seen at all. Matt's slipping a little. I'm going to have to kid him a little about that."

"You two kid each other a lot, don't you? Don't you ever hurt each other's feelings?"

Sam laughed softly. "Son, when you ride with a person as long as Matt and I have, you can get by with a lot, because you have the trust. We joke a lot, but when push comes to shove, we both know we'd fight our way into hell and fight the devil himself for each other . . . and our friends."

"I don't see Matt anymore."

"Good. I'd hate to think he forgot everything I taught him!"

"There's Mr. Brown . . . Lester. Looks like he's trying to sneak up on that one fellow."

"So, Tommy, our job is to watch and make sure nobody gets a drop on our men. If trouble happens, we would have to cover our guys. We don't want anything to happen to them."

"Even if it means killing the rustlers down there?"

"If it's them or us . . . yes. Don't ever shoot unless you have no other choice. Killing a man is never something to be taken lightly. No matter what the fight."

Tommy turned his attention back to the valley.

"Hey, Sam . . . one of the rustlers seems to be missing. The big one that we saw at first."

Sam inched forward slightly to get a better view.

"You're right, Tommy. And I don't like that. Keep your eyes open. If he doesn't show up soon . . ."

The sound of a gun being cocked suddenly sounded loudly in the afternoon air behind Sam's head.

Ash Crawford suspected something was wrong. He couldn't put his finger on it, but he could feel it. Based on what he learned from town and what Smiley told him, he would lay odds that Bodine and Two-Wolves were in the area. But where? He got his answer when he spotted a quick flash of sunlight off metal from one of the hills overlooking the valley. Would that be Bodine or Two-Wolves? If so, they weren't as smart as they were cracked up to be, revealing their presence in that way.

Ash quietly worked his way up the hill toward where he thought he had seen the sunlight glimmer off metal. He made little noise as he moved up and around. Brush interrupted his view of the valley along the path he was taking, but he could hear the cattle starting to move noisily down below. Ash didn't know cattle very well, but he figured something was disturbing them. Maybe those two strangers were out here to cause some trouble. Ash was ready for them. He figured they couldn't be as tough as Smiley had suggested since Smiley himself was a weakling. Ash still couldn't understand how the rustler could have let Lester Brown walk away a few days before. It would have been better to shoot him and be done with it. Such weakness made Ash distrustful. Who knew what Smiley would try next? Hell, he might even chicken out and hand the cattle back to Bodine and the others!

Ash moved slower now, listening carefully. He heard voices just ahead, speaking so softly that they were barely noticeable. Perhaps if he hadn't been listening, he wouldn't have even heard the whispered talk. As it was, he still couldn't understand what was being said, even though he was only a few feet away.

Ash slipped to the ground and crossed the remaining few feet on his belly, holding his gun in front of him. He moved the brush out of the way to reveal a dark-haired man and a boy looking into the valley. Ash looked cautiously around, but saw nobody else. Maybe it was just these two. It had been careless of them to be caught so easily.

Ash cocked his gun and stood.

Sam turned his head slowly. The smile that had been on his face was replaced with a frown.

"So which one are you?" Ash asked. "Bodine? Or Two-Wolves?"

"My name's Sam Two-Wolves. I'm surprised you had to ask. Most people don't get me and my partner mixed up. I'm the handsome one."

"Smart-ass, huh? I've been told that you and your partner are two tough guys. I don't see much. Where's Bodine?"

"Hell if I know. I'm not my brother's keeper."

"Yeah. You think you're tough. What are you doing up here?"

"Sight-seeing. I've heard the view is spectacular this time of year."

"Go ahead and joke. It'll be the last joke you ever made. We'll see who laughs last."

Ash lifted his gun, but the sound of a gunshot came from the valley below. Other shots followed, and then a deafening roar as the cattle started a mad rush toward the valley entrance. Ash watched as Matt took out two of the rustlers and then as Smiley mounted his horse and raced for the entrance.

"Damn, I warned him about trying to get away before the job's done!" Ash said. Without even blinking an eye, he turned his gun and shot toward the racing figure. Though it was a long shot, the bullet apparently found its target. Smiley fell forward into the saddle.

Smiley knew there was somebody behind the brush. He had gun in hand as he approached.

"I know you're there," he said. "Come on out!"

Suddenly a head popped up, but it wasn't Bodine or Two-Wolves. Instead, it was the old rancher—Lester Brown!

"I've waited a long time for this!" he yelled. "I'm going to get my cows back . . . and pay you back!"

He ran and grabbed Smiley, pulling him from his horse. He brought the gun in his hand down in a fierce blow. Smiley was temporarily dazed. He staggered backward, gun still in his hand.

"Ash was right . . . I should have killed you when I had the chance," Smiley said.

"And you need to be hanged, you two-bit rustler!"

Smiley shook his head to clear it, then rushed at Lester, pushing him back and to the ground. The steers moved around them even more fidgety than before, not liking the commotion going on around them. The other riders, realizing something was wrong, started to approach.

"Hold it right there!" Matt called out, his gun pointed at them. "Stop and throw down your guns!"

The rustlers instead of stopping spurred their horses forward and pulled their guns, firing them at the blood brother. He dived behind the bushes, spraying the air with bullets. One hit the nearest rider in the face, sending him falling to the ground. Matt kneeled and shot again, hitting the other rider in the shoulder. He kept riding past where Matt was hiding, unable to stop his horse with his shattered shoulder.

The shooting stopped the outlaws, but also had an unexpected result. The cattle, already nervous, panicked at the sound of bullets exploding so near them, and they started running. The panic spread, and in seconds a stampede had started.

The animals were heading for the valley entrance . . . and nothing was going to stand in their way!

Smiley instantly realized what was going on. The damage was already done, so he pulled his gun and shot at Lester. He missed, but the rancher hit the ground to dodge the bullet. Lester shot back, also missing. Smiley ignored the shot, rushed to his horse, and raced toward the entrance, trying to stay ahead of the crazed cattle. It would be almost impossible to turn the animals by himself; but it was a small herd, and he was going to give it a try.

Amidst the deafening roar of the stampede, the pop of a gun in the distance was almost lost. Then he felt the sudden pain in his gut and the warmth of blood soaking his shirt. He knew he had been shot as he fell face forward into the saddle.

He continued to ride, shooting his gun to try and turn the herd, but it was a losing battle. Apparently the bullet had cut an artery, for he was losing blood fast. It was now soaking his shirt and saddle, making it slippery. His mind was growing fuzzy, and he found it difficult to stay in the saddle.

The gun slipped from his hand. He used both hands to try and hold on to the saddle horn, though he no longer had any feeling in his arms or legs.

The stampeding animals kept coming closer and

closer as his grip loosened on the saddle horn, and he toppled to the ground. The earth shook as he lay, trying to move, but his legs failed him.

The last thing he thought as he saw the animals rushing toward him was, "Guess I'll never get that ranch now."

Sam was angry at himself for allowing Ash Crawford to sneak up on him. He had gotten a little too self-confident and was paying too much attention to Tommy and not enough to the dangers surrounding them. The problem now was how to correct the situation.

Ash provided the answer when he turned his attention to the activity in the valley. Sam couldn't believe his eyes as the outlaw actually turned his gun away from Sam and the boy and fired into the valley! It was an opening a mile wide. Sam didn't need any other invitation. To his credit, the boy also saw it.

Tommy turned and shot at Ash. His aim was slightly off, and the bullet went through the outlaw's shirt, grazing his chest. It still made Ash howl. He whirled and pointed his gun at the boy.

Sam grabbed Ash's arm as he fired. The shot went wild. Sam kept the arm in an iron grip and twisted with a force that could have bent an iron rod. Ash howled in pain and dropped the gun.

Ash punched at Sam with his free arm. It hit a glancing blow off Sam's shoulder, which was enough for him to loosen his grip. Ash slipped away, but not before Sam kicked out, tripping him up. He sprawled on the ground near Tommy. He reached out for the boy, grabbed him by the leg and tried to pull him near. Tommy hit the arm with his gun, breaking the grip. The gun fell, then bounced down the hill. Sam leaped and fell on the outlaw, knocking him with one blow after another.

Ash was strong and managed to shrug off the blows. With a mighty shove, he pushed Sam off him toward the edge of the hill. Ash kicked Sam in the head and pushed him closer to the edge. Sam grabbed the out- law and pulled him along. Ash clutched at the ground, trying to stay away from the edge.

Below, the shots had started a stampede. The cattle looked like a black river flowing through the sea of green grass.

Ash pulled his bowie knife, kicked loose from Sam's grip, and stood. Sam's legs were sticking awkwardly over the edge. Ash took a step closer, to be sure that he could not miss with his attack.

"So, Two-Wolves, you think you're good? This time you've lost. Goodbye to an overrated wise-ass—"

Sam suddenly rolled and pulled his own knife. He reached up and grabbed Ash's shirt, pulling him to- ward him. Ash, off balance, started to fall forward. Sam thrust his knife into the outlaw's belly as he fell. The blade went through the body and exited through the back in a grisly stream of red. Sam continued to roll, throwing Ash over the hill into the stampeding cattle below, pulling out the knife as he fell.

Sam stood, and looked down the hill as the cattle pushed their way through the valley entrance, leaving behind the mangled bodies of Ash Crawford and Ralph Smiley.

Sam said, "Let's get back to our horses. The trip out should be a lot easier than the trip in."

Chapter 17

Matt had recognized Ralph Smiley as a small-time rustler, but was still astonished as Smiley mounted his horse and raced in front of the stampeding cattle. Surely he didn't think he could turn the herd by himself? Matt was shocked when the shot was fired from the hill, striking Smiley and sending him to his death.

Matt didn't have time to think about it. He grabbed one of the rustlers' horses and started after the cattle, which were already streaming through the valley entrance. In minutes, he was also through. Lester was there, too, mounted on another of the rustlers' horses.

"Can't stop them," Lester hollered over the noise. "We can gather them later."

"I have a better idea!" Matt yelled back. "They want to run . . . let's let them run. And deliver them to King Petty's doorstep!"

"Town's not that far away . . . why not?" Lester grinned and whooped. "That's a message I'd like to deliver to Petty!"

He yelled, waved his hat, and rode after the herd, urging them to continue on rather than slowing down.

Matt rode along the other side of the herd, also making noise and pushing the cattle on. In minutes, Derrell, Sam, and Tommy caught up, riding their own horses.

"What's going on?" Sam yelled, riding beside Matt.

"We're delivering a message to King Petty!"

A smile of understanding spread across Sam's face. "By golly, we might make something of you yet!" he said, motioning to Derrell and Tommy to join him in helping to move the herd.

A time or two the animals threatened to slow down, but the group fired their guns and generally raised enough hell to keep them moving quickly until the outskirts of town were in sight.

Holt found the bottles he had stashed and sneaked out of town for a good, long drunk. That's all he felt like doing after being beaten so badly by Matt and Sam, seeing Hardesty and Cooper get killed, and knowing how Petty would react to the news that the city council had appointed Matt as marshal. If he had anyplace else to go, he would have gone. Unfortunately, he had spent his entire life in Snake Creek and had no money or talents to go elsewhere. So he got drunk instead.

Now he felt really bad. He woke up facedown in the dirt near the creek, where he had fallen down in a stupor. He was muddy. His head throbbed. He felt sick to his stomach. Holt held the bottle up to the light and found it empty. And that had been his last bottle.

The former marshal rose unsteadily to his feet. What could he do now? All he could do was return to town and hope that Petty might take pity on him.

Maybe Petty would settle for giving Holt a beating and then give him another bottle. It was really the only choice open to him.

He walked unsteadily back into town. He felt sick, and it took longer than he had planned. He wondered how long it had actually been since he had started his drunk and how Petty had reacted to the news about Matt. Surely, somebody would have told him by now? Maybe he would have had a chance to get over his mad and wouldn't be too harsh with Holt. He could only hope.

Holt made his way with shaky steps into the Black Bull Saloon, where King was sitting at his usual place. He growled at Holt and said, "About time you made it back. You've been out drinking again? Should have known. Hardesty and Cooper were killed. But that's no great loss. Thought maybe you had joined them."

"You know about Hardesty and Cooper," Holt said. "So you know about Bodine?"

"He brought the bodies in," Petty growled. "What else is there to know?"

Holt took a deep breath and blurted out, "Apparently the town council found some gumption from somewhere and fired me. They appointed Bodine in my place."

Petty jumped up so fast that he turned his chair over. He yelled, "Those sons-of-bitches! I'm going to kill them! I'm going to kill them all!" He started for the door. "And I'll start with the damned Henry Ponder—"

Before he got to the door, however, a roar started to fill the air. Conn looked out the window and said,

"King! You won't believe what's coming down the street!"

Petty could hear shots, and men yelling, and then he realized the roar was being made by over a hundred stampeding cattle. He stuck his head out the door in time to see the cattle rushing down the street, Matt and Sam in the lead, directing the cattle . . . to the saloon!

"Damn!" Petty said. "Out of the way!"

The first old cow that was in the lead set foot on the wooden front step of the saloon, and broke through. It bellowed and kept coming, pushing through the door, splintering it on its hinges. It came on in, knocking down tables and chairs. Suddenly cattle were everywhere, filling the air with their bellows, feet crashing through the floor, horns splintering the bar and the walls.

Petty and the others hurried out of the way. Petty ran down the wooden sidewalk. Conn jumped through the window. The others made their way out the best they could.

After several minutes, the cattle slowed their pace and started to wander aimlessly through the trashed building. In the street, Matt, Sam, and the Browns were laughing hysterically at the sight. Petty was also surprised to see the Brandom boy with the group. He was sitting farther back, behind the others, but was also laughing.

"Hey, Petty! What do you think of this?" Lester taunted. "Got my cattle back! Just wanted to let you know that!"

"I'll kill you! I'll kill you all!"

* * *

Lilly heard the fuss, as did the rest of the town, who came out to see what was going on. A crowd quickly formed as word spread about the incident at the Black Bull. Lilly knew she was supposed to stay out of sight, but she rushed out of the store, hoping to see her friends and son safe. She breathed a sigh of relief when she saw Tommy sitting straight and tall—and apparently unhurt—on his horse, with Derrell close beside him.

The woman also laughed when she saw what the group had done to King Petty's hangout.

Sam got off his horse and stood in front of Petty. "If you want to kill somebody, try me," he said. "You seem to like going after unarmed men, women, and children. Let's see how you do against somebody who's as big as you are."

King stood motionless, his hand a safe distance away from his gun. "I understand this town has a new marshal. I want to file a complaint. My property's been destroyed and I'm being assaulted by this man!"

Matt drawled, "Well, I am wearing the badge now, and I don't see anything wrong. True, these cattle got a little out of hand, but it's no crime for cattle to run. And Sam is just carrying on a polite conversation. No law against that!"

"So what's it going to be, Petty?" Sam continued. "Are you really a coward?"

The crowd watched expectantly, waiting to see what Petty would do. He couldn't just stand and do nothing. So he lashed out with a vicious right. Except that Sam was no longer there. He stepped to one side, caught the fist, and twisted. The pressure forced Petty to the ground.

Petty freed himself from the hand clasped around his arm and rose slowly to his feet. He stood with feet slightly spread, started to reach for his gun, but stopped when he saw the look in Sam's face and his hand dropping toward the Colt.

Petty took a deep breath. "Not now," Petty said. "But your time is coming, Sam Two-Wolves. Your time is coming."

"I'll be waiting," Sam said. "Be sure to send me an invitation."

Petty dusted himself off, and turned his back to Sam as he led his men down the street. Holt lurched along behind them.

Lilly ran out into the street. Tommy slid off his horse into his mother's arms.

"I told you we'd bring him back safe and sound," Sam said. "The little show here was thrown in for free!"

The small group had turned into a larger group as they had dinner at Charlie's restaurant.

"This is a great day!" Charlie said. "Matt, I'll make my promise good. Your meal is on the house—and so are the meals for all our friends! The stranglehold that King Petty had on this town is broken!"

The others muttered agreements, but Matt held up his hands to silence the group.

"We've put a crimp in Petty's style, but he's not defeated yet. Not until he's dead. I thought for a moment this afternoon that he was going to go for his gun against Sam, only he decided to live a little longer. It is only a matter of time before Petty tries something, and then we'll nail him. You can bet it'll be something sneaky and underhanded. So everybody shouldn't let their guard down. Charlie, that's especially true for you, Henry, and other members of the council. It took a lot of courage to go against him that way."

"It wasn't us. We had faith in you. And Sam."

"I know you won't shoot Petty in cold blood, though he deserves it," Lilly said. "That's not your way. But why not arrest him? He's surely committed enough crimes to put him away? And you now have the authority."

Matt spooned another piece of pie onto his plate. Sam said, "Hey, pass that down here before you hog it all!"

"I'm the marshal," Matt pointed out. "That gives me a certain amount of privilege!"

Sam responded by cutting a bigger piece of pie and slipping it onto his plate.

Matt explained, "Petty's committed more crimes than I could count, but it would take time to collect evidence and go through the proper judicial route. And there's no guarantee he wouldn't get out of jail and come back for you and the others. What we're doing is giving him some rope so that he can hang himself, solving the problem once and for all."

"I don't want to be a prisoner here for the rest of my life," Lilly said. "No offense, Clarissa—you've been wonderful!"

"No offense taken."

"As good as Clarissa and Henry have been to me— as good as all of you have been to me—I still want to go home. I want to get on with my life, and there's lots of work that needs doing out there."

"You need to be someplace safe," Sam cautioned.

"I'll stay with her and Tommy," Derrell said. "I admit I'm not the best fighter or shooter, but between the three of us we could probably hold our own. I doubt if much could happen without you and Sam knowing about it, since you're staying in town to keep an eye on Petty. If he tries something, I know you'd also be out at Lilly's place in a flash." Derrell turned to Lilly. "That is, if that would be all right with you?"

"You're always welcome out there," she responded.

"Great!" Tommy said. "Could Mr. Brown . . . Lester . . . come too?"

"I've got to take care of our own place—now that we got our cattle back," Lester said. "But I'll also be close by, if needed. Don't you worry about that!"

"Then it's settled," Lilly said, folding her hands in her lap. "I'll be going home after dinner!"

Matt forked out another piece of pie, cleaning out the pan. "Well, the lady's spoken!" he said. "I've learned never to argue with a lady. So guess the matter's settled!"

Later, after Matt and Sam had quietly made sure that Derrell, Lilly, and Tommy were safely on their way back to the homestead, the two blood brothers talked softly among themselves as they watched the saloon where King Petty had moved his operations.

"Lilly's still not out of danger," Sam said.

"I know," Matt said. "But they'll probably be as safe at home as anywhere. Derrell will take good care of her and the boy."

Sam chuckled. "Yeah. He's taking a personal interest in them. It's like he's already part of the family."

"Can't blame him," Matt said. "It might be nice to be a part of a family like that."

"Maybe," Sam agreed. "Let's make sure that we take care of Petty so that they can live happily ever after."

"You've got that right. Petty will make his move soon. But what will that crazy sonofabitch try next?"

Chapter 18

King Petty threw his glass across the room, hitting Holt in the face. This building was not as nice as the Black Bull Saloon had been. This had faded wood, a warped bar, a dirty mirror behind the bar. It was located almost outside of town. It was as if the outlaw gang was being forced out of town, and it was making Petty crazy.

The whiskey glass shattered, cutting Holt. He screamed in pain, clutching his bleeding face. Petty leaped up from the table and pushed the other man out of his way to the floor.

"Damn Two-Wolves and Bodine! Damn this whole town! Damn all of you! And especially damn that bitch and that stupid kid." He stomped around the room, kicking Holt from time to time as he went by. The others watched in morbid fascination, hoping that his anger wouldn't be directed next at them. "Well, am I right? Or am I wrong?"

The others looked silently at each other, not wanting to be the first to talk.

Petty yelled, "Well, what is it? Am I right? Answer me!"

Conn, his tall body leaning against the bar, was the only one that dared to answer. He said, "I'd say you have good reason to be pissed. Those two yahoos come marching into town and try to take over. Stealing your cattle and stampeding them through town and into the Black Bull that way. And the townspeople are just as bad, removing your man—such as he is—from office and making Bodine the marshal. And damned if the first thing Bodine does is to allow Two-Wolves to attack you in front of the whole town, just because we threatened the boy. That whole bunch needs to be taken down some notches."

"Damned right! They can't treat me that way!"

Holt, on the floor, had managed to crawl out of the way. Petty's kick this time missed its mark.

"Here's an idea," Conn suggested. "If we really wanted to, we could probably take down Bodine and Two-Wolves. When they're gone, you can take care of the rest of the turncoats in this town at your own pace. But that's probably too good for them. They really need to be strung up and left for the vultures."

The others in the room murmured agreement, but nobody stepped forward to volunteer.

"Hanging's too good for them," Petty yelled, even louder, slamming his fist on the table. "I *really* want to hurt them."

"Then let's hit them where it hurts the most," Conn continued, rolling a whiskey glass between his palms. "That Brandom woman apparently thinks the world of her kid. And for some reason Two-Wolves and

Bodine have also taken a liking to him. Why don't we make an example of *him.*"

Petty stopped his pacing and glared at Conn. "What do you mean?"

"Let's string the boy up."

Holt, on the floor, could barely believe his ears. He had seen Petty kill men for little or no reason, but never a boy. Somehow that seemed different. The room grew silent, but Petty's eyes grew bright.

"Hell, why didn't I think of that?" he said, suddenly calm. He spoke in a normal tone of voice, and he almost seemed cheerful. "I still plan to have that woman—after all the trouble she's put me through, I damned well deserve it! But it would sure teach her and her friends a lesson before they die."

"I don't have any love lost for that boy, myself," Conn said. "He was riding with the bunch when they attacked us and stole your cattle right under Smiley's nose and destroyed the saloon."

"But he's just a kid!" Holt said, trying to stand. He was holding on to the bar, pulling himself up.

Petty pulled his gun, stepped over to Holt, and put the barrel to his head. The former marshal closed his eyes tightly, trying not to shake. Petty cocked the gun. It sounded very loud in the small, dingy room.

The seconds seemed like an eternity, until Petty laughed.

"I'll be damned. You're not begging me for your life. Will wonders never cease?" Petty uncocked the gun and hit it against the side of Holt's head. He collapsed to the floor in a daze. "No never mind to me how old that brat is. Just like I don't care about you, Holt, or anybody else in this damned town. I'm King

Petty, and I'll do what I want. Don't you or anybody else ever forget that!"

"Want me to get the boys together?" Conn asked.

"Get to it. We've got some business to attend to!"

Clarissa Ponder paused at the front door of the store, ready to open it to start the day's business, and waved to Matt as he walked down the street. It was rather odd to see a real law officer in town again after all the years of King Petty running the show and with a succession of men like Holt in the marshal position. So far, he and Sam had managed to stay on top, but Petty wasn't like most men. He was crazy. But Matt and Sam could do the job if anybody could.

She wished them luck, and not just for the town's sake. In the short time she had known the two men, she had grown to like them, and she hated the thought of something bad happening to them.

Clarissa felt rather than heard movement behind her, but it was a welcome presence. She turned her head slightly and said, "Good morning, Sam."

"And good morning to you, Clarissa."

"What brings you out and about so early?"

Sam followed the woman into the store. She picked up her apron from behind the counter and put it on. Sam said, "I need some . . . coffee."

"Already used up what you bought the other day?" Clarissa smiled. "That's all right, Sam. You can never have too much coffee."

Sam laughed softly. "You're a pretty smart woman. I guess I mainly just wanted to come by and visit awhile. I've been thinking about how you took care of

Lilly the other day, and that tea you made. It reminded me of something my mother used to make, that she learned from—"

Clarissa touched Sam gently on the arm.

"I'll share something with you that nobody in town knows about, except for my husband. I am part Cherokee. I learned some of the old ways when I was a kid . . . before I chose to join the white man's world."

"You ever regret it?"

"Not often. I made the decision, and then I met Henry. I've had a good life. I suppose if we would have had children, I might have wondered how much of my Indian heritage I wanted to pass down. But the only child we had died when he was a baby, so it was never really a question."

Sam leaned against the counter, looking thoughtful.

"That's the thing about life. The trick is to live the best life you can. But sometimes it's tough knowing what's the right thing to do."

"I don't intend to stick my nose in where it doesn't belong, but I think doing the right thing is very important to you. Is that why you jumped in and helped Lilly?"

"I thought it was a clever way to meet a pretty woman!"

"Go ahead and joke, Sam. But I know better."

Sam grew more serious and said, "All right, I'll admit it. I make no secret of the fact that I'm Cheyenne, but for reasons of my own I live the life I am. I've seen an awful lot of things that weren't right in this world. I know that most of them I can't do anything about. A few things I can do something about, and I'll do my damndest to make right what I can make right."

"You're a good man, Sam. That fact will shape everything you do in your life. I know that sometimes you'll have doubts and problems, and some of them nobody will fully understand—not even Matt. And possibly not even the woman you marry—"

Sam held up his hands and said, "Now, wait a minute!"

"—if you marry someday. And you probably will. The point I'm trying to make, though, is that no matter what you do, you should not deny who you are. You will always have the blood of your parents flowing through you. You will always have your heritage to fall back on. Keep that in mind as you decide what is the right thing. I think it will serve you well. This situation with King Petty is a good example."

"I'm not sure what you mean."

"Most men would never have gotten involved to start with. But because of who you are, you came to Lilly's aid. Most men would have felt fear and not stuck around to face Petty. I can tell, though, that you've come from a long line of warriors. I'd be willing to bet your father was a leader of your people. He passed his courage on to you. I know you will face Petty, and any other problem that comes your way, with bravery. That is something very rare and special."

Sam smiled and took Clarissa's hand.

"Thanks for being so straight with me. I can always count on Matt being honest with me—even brutally so. That's why I can trust him so much. But you said some things that even he might have a difficult time saying."

"I know that you and Matt have a special bond. But sometimes even that is not enough." She grinned. "Do you still want that coffee?"

"Of course! If I don't come out with something, everybody's going to wonder what I've been doing here all this time with the prettiest woman in town!"

"You are a charmer, Sam Two-Wolves." She prepared the coffee and handed it to Sam. "I don't need to tell you that King Petty is out there waiting for you. And I know you will be careful. But please remember that your efforts are appreciated. Anything Henry or I could do . . ."

Sam took the coffee. "You've already done it, Clarissa. You've already done it."

Matt walked down the street in the sunlight, and waved to Clarissa Ponder as she prepared to open the store for the day. He noticed Sam walking softly behind her. Matt was glad to see Sam talking to her. Matt had thought his blood brother had been kind of moody at times recently, but couldn't figure out what to do about it. From what Matt had seen of the woman, she seemed to have some kind of understanding that might help. Sam followed Clarissa into the store, and Matt continued his stroll down the town's main street.

Matt had been in his new job as City Marshal of Snake Creek for only a short time, but so far all had remained quiet. He knew, of course, that it wouldn't last. Matt and Sam had brought the fight to King

Petty, humiliating him in front of the town not just once but several times. Petty would be almost crazy with anger. He had proven himself capable of doing anything. The question was, what would he now do in retaliation? Derrell Brown had been left behind at Lilly's—he seemed to be hitting it off well with the widow and her boy, and Matt was content to let him look after things on the farm.

The new marshal's walk led him past the ruins of the Black Bull Saloon. The ground in front where the stampeding cattle had churned it up remained a mess. Matt smiled at the surprise on Petty's face as he'd rushed out of the building just ahead of the cattle. Maybe it was a dirty trick to play on the town, but most of the people had seemed to enjoy the show.

"This place is in one helluva shape, isn't it?" Sam said from behind Matt.

"Looks like a herd of stampeding cattle ran through it," Matt agreed, with a straight face.

"Wonder who would have allowed such a thing?"

"Don't know. Think I should try to find out and run them in?"

Sam made a clucking sound with his tongue. "Isn't that just like you? Give you a badge, and you start wanting to throw people in jail! Guess I should have warned them!"

"You're just jealous because they picked me instead of you! Guess I could deputize you . . ."

"And work for you! You think I'm crazy or something?"

"Do you really want me to answer that question?"

"Come to think of it . . . no."

Sam fell into place beside Matt as they walked down

the street. In spite of the friendly banter, they both knew Petty would try something soon, and they wanted to be ready for it.

To Matt, Sam seemed a little more at ease than he had been. Any other person might not have noticed it, but Matt knew his partner better than anybody.

"You and Clarissa have a good talk?"

Sam held up the small paper bag. "I got the coffee I needed," he said.

Matt smiled and said, "Glad to hear it." The two men walked a little farther until they came to an alley. "Let's run by Petty's new place."

"Sure. Life's been almost too boring for the past, oh . . . ten minutes or so."

The alley was deserted, and the small, faded building that housed the dingy saloon at the end of the alley also seemed deserted.

"How do you like that?" Matt asked. "Nobody's home."

Sam scanned the ground. "I don't like it. A lot of men were here, and left fast. Not more than an hour ago."

A groan came from inside the building.

"Sounds like somebody's hurt," Matt said. "You go around back. I'll go in the front. Let's check this out."

Sam didn't say a word, but disappeared around the corner of the building. Matt pulled his Colt and moved silently through the door. At first, he saw nothing, but heard another moan. He stepped inside and saw the figure leaning, trying to pull himself up to the bar, clutching at an almost empty whiskey bottle.

"Holt? What are you doing?"

Matt stepped closer as Sam came in through the

back. Matt leaned down to talk with the former marshal and looked him over. The other man groaned and took a drink.

"Petty sure did a number on you this time," Matt said softly. "Hell, you're nothing but black and blue."

"He was going to kill me," Holt said. "I don't know why he didn't pull the trigger. He had the gun to my head."

"What's going on?" Sam demanded. "Where's Petty?"

Holt looked over at Sam and said slowly, "They're going after the boy. This time to string him up."

"Is even King Petty that cruel and vicious?" Matt asked.

Sam's eyes grew hard. "Like hell he is," he said, already running for the door.

Matt let Holt fall back to the floor and followed Sam.

Chapter 19

Derrell Brown, in spite of the inherent dangers, was enjoying the day. He had lost Lilly once before when she had married Jack Brandom. After she was married, she was no longer eligible, so he'd tried to put her out of his mind. Now, because of the terrible tragedy in her life, he had another chance to be with her. He would not have wanted Jack Brandom killed under any circumstances, but he was more than willing to help Lilly with no thought of repayment. To him, being with Lilly was payment enough.

The task that Sam had assigned him now was to watch after Lilly and Tommy, in case King Petty tried to pull anything. Derrell had done well so far, periodically checking the area around the house and making sure the home and outbuildings were secure. He wasn't sure what he would do if Petty actually showed up. He did know he would not back down. He would fight to the death for Lilly and her son.

Lilly had spread a cloth under the tree in the front yard and had brought some biscuits and fried meat out for a little picnic in the spring sunshine. Derrell was leaning against the tree with Tommy beside him. He smiled at the unexpectedly domestic scene that made even a hint of danger seem a thousand miles away.

"This is great," Derrell said. "I've never seen anything like this. Does your mom do this often?"

"Not really," Tommy said. "When my dad . . . was alive . . . she never did this. He didn't like eating outside much. I like it. It's kind of fun."

"Fun? Seems sometimes that I've eaten most of my meals outside."

"You're lucky."

Derrell laughed. "Lucky? I don't know. Most of those meals were eaten on the run, as I chased down or worked with cattle. It's paid off . . . we got a good herd going. We almost lost it, but thanks to Matt and Sam we've got our animals back. Still, there's lots of work ahead of us. It's not an easy life being a cowboy."

"Will you show me how to ride? And rope? I'd like to work with you. Would you teach me?"

Derrell felt an unexpected closeness to the boy. "We'll talk to your mom about it," he said. "First thing to do is to make sure you guys remain safe. As long as King Petty is around, nobody is safe."

Lilly called from the house, "Tommy, would you help me?"

"Sure, Mom!"

Tommy ran into the house. A minute later, he came out, followed by Lilly carrying a bowl. Derrell stepped up and took the bowl from her, saying, "Here, let me help you with that."

The woman smiled, and they sat on the ground.

"I don't know how I could ever thank you," Lilly said. "You've done so much for Tommy and me."

"I haven't done that much," Derrell protested. "Nothing any other man wouldn't have done. And, to be honest, I'm a little concerned about Petty. It's been too quiet. He won't quit until he gets his way . . . or dies trying. And we know how tough it'd be to kill him. Even with Sam and Matt on our side."

"We'll be fine . . . you'll see."

Derrell was very aware of the woman just a few feet from him, but his eyes were on the distant hills, trying to watch for any signs of danger. He poured some molasses in his plate and sopped a biscuit in it.

"I've been wanting to ask you something," Derrell said hesitantly. "I know you've got a lot on your mind and so on . . . but . . ."

"Yes?"

"Tommy asked if he could ride with me, learn a little about cattle and ranching . . ."

"I don't see why not. As long as he gets his chores done around here."

"Thanks, Mom!"

"It'd be good for him to learn different kinds of work. And I imagine he'd like spending time with you."

Lilly smiled, so Derrell continued, "And there's something else, too."

"Yes?"

"Maybe after some time passes . . . and things get settled out . . . and this Petty thing is taken care of . . . could I . . ." Derrell cleared his throat. "Could I maybe come by sometimes and see you."

"I'd like that."

"I mean, that is if you don't mind . . ." He paused. "You'd like that?"

"Give me a little time to work things out in my head . . . but sure. I'd enjoy that."

In the corral near the barn, the horses started to pace restlessly and whinnied. Normally, it might have meant nothing, but Derrell was going to take no chances.

"In the house, get your gun ready," Derrell said. "Do it, now!"

Lilly and Tom jumped up and headed for the door, but it was already too late.

A dozen riders, all wearing masks, galloped over the small hill, hooves stamping on the grave, guns blazing.

Sam was worried and he felt guilty. He had left the woman and child alone, and even with Derrell's help they might have a difficult time dealing with Petty. He had been certain that he or Matt would be able to keep track of the gang in town. It was a miscalculation that Sam hoped wouldn't be fatal.

Sam led the way, though Matt kept pace. Neither had to check the trail to know where the Petty gang was headed. The only question was, could the blood brothers get to Lilly's in time to save the boy?

"How much head start do you think they have?" Matt yelled out, making his voice heard over the wind.

"Maybe twenty minutes, more or less," Sam hollered back. "No matter. It's too long!"

"We'll make it. Petty won't win this one!"

"I should have stayed with Lilly . . . Derrell will have a tough time with that bunch . . ."

"Don't blame yourself! You know that they're as safe as they can be."

"I probably should have kept them close to us!"

"You know Lilly wouldn't stand for that! You couldn't keep her prisoner!"

"I wish we could have kept her safer!"

Sam's face grew grim, his eyes harder, as he lowered his head into the wind and spurred his horse to greater speed.

The outlaws were on Derrell, Lilly, and Tommy almost before they could react. Lilly had Tommy by the hand, and they were halfway to the door when the first riders galloped into the yard. One pair of strong hands reached out and swooped up Tommy and lifted him from the ground. Lilly screamed, and tried to hit at the outlaw.

Conn laughed and kept on riding, the boy's legs dangling behind him.

Lilly screamed again, then remembered the gun in her apron. She reached down, clutched at it, but was interrupted by another set of hands grabbing her and pulling her off the ground. She tried to turn, but could not. Instead, she found herself pushed roughly facedown across the saddle in front of the rider. She didn't have to look to know that it was King Petty who had seized her. No mask could disguise his identity.

She tried to wriggle free, to get a firm grasp on the gun, but Petty held her too tightly. She just could not get the weapon in her hand.

Lilly felt dirty just from his touch and wanted desperately to get away. From the angle she was facing,

Lilly could not see her son, and she was worried about him. She couldn't even see Derrell. Lilly wanted to scream again, but her throat was dry, making it impossible to even wet her lips.

Derrell had seen the riders approach, pulled his gun and managed to squeeze off several shots. One of his bullets hit one of the outlaws; but he did not have the speed or accuracy of Sam, and the thug just kept coming.

Derrell refused to step aside. He aimed more carefully, steadied his arm, and squeezed off a shot. This time, the bullet hit its target. The slug entered the outlaw's chest, causing a splotch of red to appear on the shirt. He opened his mouth in surprise, but no sound came out. The man tried to raise his gun for another shot, but his fingers no longer worked. The gun slipped from his hand, and the outlaw fell from the saddle.

The horse kept coming at Derrell. He tried to step out of the way at the last instant, but was sideswiped by the animal. He was knocked to the ground, the wind knocked out of him. Derrell rolled over to his knees, and started to stand, when the other outlaws arrived. Two of them slid off their horses and picked Derrell up, pinning his arms behind him. Horrified, he watched as Conn held the boy and Petty forced Lilly down on the saddle in front of him.

Derrell struggled, but was unable to get away.

The riders made several passes around the house and came back to report to Petty.

"Nobody else here," one said.

"Everything's clear," another said.

Petty nudged his horse forward, stopping in front of Derrell.

"How nice," he said. "Looks like we interrupted a little dinner here."

"Seems like you and your men are good at that," Derrell answered.

Petty kicked, hitting Derrell in the face with the toe of his boot. Blood gushed from Derrell's nose.

"Smart-ass. Just answer the questions. Where are the others? Bodine and Two-Wolves?"

"They're around," Derrell said. "Just wait a few minutes. You'll see them soon enough."

Petty kicked again, threw the woman from the saddle and leaped to the ground. He punched Derrell repeatedly until he was barely conscious as the other men held him helpless. Finally, Petty said, "Let him go."

The two men stepped back. Petty started to walk away, then unexpectedly pivoted, pulling his gun,

Lilly screamed, "No . . . not again!"

Petty ignored her and fired. The bullet struck Derrell, spinning him around to the ground.

Lilly finally pulled the gun from her apron pocket, but Petty was ahead of her. He grabbed her arm with one hand and took the gun with his other hand.

"Sorry, Widow. Guns aren't for women to play with." Petty laughed. "I have something else for you!"

She looked around, trying to get herself oriented. Derrell was motionless on the ground. Where was her son?

"Why don't you just leave us alone? Haven't you done enough to us?"

"Not enough to suit me!" Petty continued to laugh.

"Or, unsuit me, if you will!" He pulled down his mask, putting his face close to hers. "I've been through hell because of you, Widow. I aim to enjoy you!"

The others laughed with him.

"What about the boy?" a harsh voice called out.

"Let's take care of him first. Give the widow a show. Then I'll get down to the real business at hand! Bring the brat over here. By the tree."

The big man holding Tommy rode his horse slowly toward the center of the yard, then threw the boy to the ground. Tommy stood, staring at Petty and Conn.

"Hand me the rope," Petty ordered.

Conn reached into his saddlebags and pulled out a rope already tied in a hangman's noose.

"I already took the liberty of preparing it," Conn said. "Hope you don't mind, King?"

"Good man. You did a good job." Petty walked around the boy and the tree, kicking what was left of the picnic out of the way. "This is a good sturdy tree. It should do the job." He tossed the rope around an overhanging limb, adjusting it so that the noose dangled freely. "Bring the boy here."

Rough hands pushed Tommy toward Petty. He half stumbled, but managed to keep his balance. Petty yanked the boy toward him. Lilly lunged forward, but two of the others jerked her so strongly that her head snapped back. They leered at her as she struggled.

"Leave the boy alone!" she yelled. "I'll give you anything you want!"

"You will, anyway," Petty said. He placed the noose around the boy's neck, pulled it snug, and tied the other end around the saddle horn of his horse. "You all deserve this. It will be a pleasure to watch you die."

Lilly struggled some more. For the first time in her life, she yelled out profanities at Petty. He ignored her and put his hand on the horse, ready to slap its rump and send the boy to his death.

Chapter 20

Matt Bodine and Sam Two-Wolves had been in many races against time in their adventures together. The stakes in some of those contests were their very lives. This race was different in that the life of a young boy was at stake.

The two blood brothers rode faster than they had ever gone before. The countryside was a blur as they made a direct line to the Brandom homestead.

"Almost there!" Matt yelled. "How are we doing?"

"We're catching up to them!" Sam yelled back. "Those tracks were made just minutes ago!"

Matt was a good tracker, but even he had to give credit to Sam. Nobody else he had ever known would have been able to know so many details from just a few tracks, especially while on the back of a racing horse. With Sam, it was almost as much instinct as training.

Matt also kicked his horse into greater speed, and for a second pulled slightly ahead of Sam. Through the trees, the two blood brothers could see the outlaws near the house.

"I'm going to circle around the back way," Matt said.

Sam acknowledged the comment by pushing his horse even faster.

Matt had no plan. In a situation like this, there was no way to plan. A person could only jump in and think on his feet, making things happen as best he could.

Sam crossed the hill where Jack was buried. The first thing he noticed was the gang of outlaws gathered together in Lilly's front yard. The second thing he noticed was the rope hanging over the tree limb with the noose on the other end around Tommy's neck. He was almost too far away.

Suddenly, Matt's horse burst around the barn, though Matt was no longer on its back! It was an unusual distraction, but it did the job. The horse sprinted into the group, sending the thugs scattering. The confusion lasted only for a few seconds, but it was enough for Sam to gain additional precious feet.

Sam pulled his Colt and fired. It was an almost impossible shot, even for Sam, though he came close. The slug whistled past Petty's ear. He was startled and pulled his own gun. Sam continued to race toward him. Realizing his mistake, Petty changed the revolver to his other hand and raised his arm.

His hand came down solidly on the horse's rump. The horse jumped, tightening the hanging rope.

From the barn came a rebel yell and a flying figure. Matt ran and leaped from the hay loft, landing next to the horse. He grabbed at the halter and tried to hold it back with sheer strength. The horse, scared amidst all the noise and confusion, started to buck. Matt held on tightly, hoping to create some slack in the rope.

Sam was now so close that Petty could see the dark eyes blazing through him. Sam holstered his gun, then reached for the large knife he always carried. Petty figured Sam would try to cut him as he passed.

Petty shifted position, crouched and shot.

The bullet whistled through empty air as Sam leaped from the horse's back, sailing over Petty.

Sam grabbed hold of the tree limb with one hand and sliced at the rope with the other. The razor-sharp blade almost instantly severed the rope. Tommy, who had been forced to his tiptoes, fell to the ground.

A dozen men swarmed over the two blood brothers.

Matt was paying most of his attention to the thousand pounds of horseflesh trying to bite, kick, and buck him off. He could not make out clearly who his attackers were, but didn't hesitate an instant. He raised his boots and allowed the horse to put the force behind the kicks. One of the men backed away with a broken jaw. A second man lay moaning on the ground after he was kicked in the groin. A third man narrowly escaped as a hoof grazed his head.

The remaining outlaws gave Matt and the thrashing horse a wide berth, when Matt suddenly let go of the animal. He rolled along the ground, coming up with a Colt in his hand. His gun blazed, doubling over one of the thugs and sending the others running for cover.

King Petty didn't like what he was seeing. For the first time in his life, his wishes were being successfully opposed. It was as if Sam and Matt had somehow materialized out of thin air to thwart his plans.

He watched as his men were taken out. They were

all tough men, thugs who in some cases were almost as violent as him. Yet, they were being taken out by the two blood brothers as if they were nothing.

Sam cut down the boy and looked straight at Petty. The outlaw had never seen such a look of rage and anger that was now in Sam's face. The eyes seemed to burn through him. Petty shot at Sam, who had already leaped to the ground.

Petty turned and saw Conn taking the woman from the other two men. Behind him more of his men were running toward Sam. If they were trying to escape, they were going in the wrong direction.

"Let me have her," Petty growled. He grabbed Lilly and pulled her roughly from Conn's grasp.

"Sure, King . . . whatever you want."

"I'm getting out of here. Maybe those two bastards cheated me out of everything else, but they're not taking the woman away from me."

"Are you crazy? She'd just slow you down."

"Get out of my way!" Petty screamed. He grabbed a horse, threw the woman onto the saddle and jumped up behind her.

Conn felt the hot lead flying around him. He decided that retreat in this case would be the wisest action. He found the nearest horse and took off just seconds behind Petty.

Petty wasn't sure where he could go. He knew that there was no place he could go that he would be safe. Sam would find him and try to kill him for what he had tried to do. Even if he could find a way to escape Sam, now that Matt was a sworn-in lawman, he could bring in the law from all over the country to search for him. For all Petty knew, he may have even violated federal laws.

No matter. He was King Petty. He had owned the area around Snake Creek for years. He would find a way to still get what he wanted, when he wanted.

Now he wanted the woman. And he would have her.

He headed for Snake Creek, thinking he might lose any pursuers in its shallow water.

Sam could see the action clearly from where he was holding on to the tree limb, but didn't wait around for anybody to start using him for target practice. He spotted Conn with Lilly and saw King racing toward them. With a knife in his free hand, Sam could not get his gun clear of its holster and fire soon enough. He swung toward the small group, landing lightly on his feet, right in front of four outlaws running toward him.

All had guns, but seemed unnerved to find two hundred pounds of fury standing before them, knife gleaming in the sunlight. At that time, in spite of his short hair and western garb, he looked like his ancestors had during the height of battle—an Indian warrior out for blood. The outlaws had their guns in hand, but hesitated for an instant before shooting.

It was an instant too long.

Sam's knife flashed, and the unlucky outlaw closest to him fell to the ground with a slash in him from his neck to his shoulder. As his blood started to stain the ground, Sam thrust in the opposite direction, opening a wound in the guts of a second outlaw.

The other two outlaws finally regained their senses

and started shooting. Terrified of the figure before them, they fired wildly, emptying their guns without hitting anything but dirt. Sam kept coming at them, and with two quick swipes they were history, faces down to the ground, guns motionless in their lifeless hands.

Sam was barely breathing hard, looking to take on anybody else foolish enough to stand in his way.

Except suddenly no other outlaws were left alive and standing.

Matt stood, his gun still in hand. Though his back was to Sam, he knew exactly where his partner stood and what he was doing. He worked his way slowly backward toward Sam.

Sam also backed toward Matt so that they would meet in the middle of the yard, under the tree. They were ready for an attack from any direction.

Sam kneeled down and talked softly to Tommy.

"Are you all right, boy?" he asked.

Tommy rubbed his neck and tried to smile. The words came out in a choke.

"I'm still alive," Tommy said. "What about Derrell? They shot him."

Sam helped Tommy lean against the tree and looked at the bodies scattered around the yard.

Derrell Brown was not among them.

"They may have shot him, but I reckon they didn't kill him," Sam suggested. "Unless a body can get up and walk away. I don't see him here now."

"Two others that aren't here," Matt said. "The mighty King is gone. Along with Lilly. Also his crony, Conn. I was trying to get a bead on them, but it wasn't possible holding on to that bronc."

"I saw them, but from where I was hanging couldn't get a shot, either," Sam said.

"We saved the boy, and that was the most important thing at the time," Matt said. He looked around. "Damned, I didn't see which way they went."

A running horse was heard from around the barn. Matt and Sam both turned instantly, guns at the ready, but dropped them to their sides when they saw it was a friend, not an enemy.

Lester Brown galloped into view.

"I've been trying to stay close," he explained. "I know Derrell can take care of himself, but I didn't want to take chances. I heard the shooting and . . ." He whistled. "Damned, you boys work fast. I'm glad you all ain't enemies of mine."

Sam's eyes scanned the ground. "I've got the trail. I'm going after Petty. He's mine."

"Only if you get to him first," Matt said.

"You can count on it." Sam leaped onto his horse's back and galloped down the path toward the creek.

Matt quickly found his own horse and mounted.

"Lester, stay here and look after the boy," Matt said. "We'll be back, Tommy. And we'll have your mom. You can count on it."

Lester put his hand on the boy's shoulder as the two blood brothers disappeared from sight.

Chapter 21

Derrell hurt, and he hurt bad. He wasn't sure where he had taken the slug, though most of the pain seemed to come from his leg. He gritted his teeth and tried to fight off the waves of nausea and blackness that threatened to engulf him. He felt sick inside. He had failed Lilly and the boy. He had let King Petty surprise them and defeat them. Derrell, however, was still alive and planned to do *something*.

He lay on the ground in pain, hearing the gunshots and the fight. With great effort, he finally pushed himself up from the ground. His head cleared enough to see Matt and Sam destroying Petty's men.

And then he saw Lilly. He was suddenly awake and clearly saw the action as Petty yanked the woman from Conn's grip, threw her onto a horse, and mounted behind her.

Derrell tried to ignore the pain in his leg and stood. His movement was almost unnoticed amidst the chaos going on around him. One of Petty's men rode by, his eyes on Sam and his knife. Derrell pulled the rider from his horse and grabbed the reins and saddle. The horse, already anxious from all the commotion, tried to run. Derrell held on and pulled himself onto the saddle, finally finding the stirrups.

He followed Petty and the woman.

Petty moved fast, but Derrell had been riding this land since he was a kid. Even with the pain stabbing at him, Derrell knew every hill, gully, and creek. He managed to gain ground on the outlaw.

Petty seemed to be headed for Snake Creek, from which the town had gained its name. Derrell couldn't figure out why Petty was going in that direction, unless he had some vague idea of losing his tracks in the water. It seemed like a stupid idea to Derrell, but then Petty had always been more concerned with killing and raping than with learning the land. If he had taken the time to learn, Petty would have realized that if the spring sun had warmed up the land enough, it would be bad news for the outlaw. This did not concern Derrell. What did worry him was the woman that Petty had kidnapped.

Derrell glanced down at his leg and saw the fresh blood soaking his pants. He still wasn't sure how badly he was shot, but he knew that he couldn't keep going much longer if he kept losing blood.

He took a gamble. He knew a shortcut to the creek. He decided to take it, hoping to catch Petty there.

Derrell turned the horse and urged it forward with his good leg. A wave of blackness tried to engulf him, but he managed to stay in the saddle.

In minutes, he had pushed through the thick underbrush and saw the waters of Snake Creek. It looked cool and inviting. At certain times of the year it was a good place to fish, as Matt and Sam had found out. At other times, it was a good place to avoid. Sometimes even natives didn't know when those times would be.

Derrell passed the former camp where Matt and Sam had had their fishing trip interrupted by Petty's men. That time now seemed a long time ago.

Petty suddenly came into view, not bothering to slow his horse as it waded into the creek.

Behind him was Sam, his gun drawn and ready to shoot.

Conn was not particularly loyal to any man. He had joined up with King Petty because he knew a good thing when he saw it. In many ways, he and Petty were cut from the same kind of cloth. As long as it suited his needs, he followed Petty's wishes. Now that Petty had lost—and lost big—Conn decided it was time to move on. It was the pattern that had always worked for him before.

He pushed his horse hard for several miles, then slowed down, feeling he was out of danger. He stopped, dismounted, and took inventory of his situation. He had some money and a few supplies in his saddlebags, since he was always prepared to make a quick move, if necessary. He had a good horse and his guns. He had made a clean getaway.

Conn whistled softly.

"What are you so happy about? Didn't think you'd really get away, did you?"

The outlaw turned with hands in the air. Matt was standing, legs spread apart, his gun still in its holster.

"So. Matthew Bodine. Why are you following me? King Petty is the man you should be after."

"Sam will take care of him. If there's anything left of Petty, I can arrest him later. I'm going to bring you in for the principle of the thing. I know you've been involved with Petty's operations. I'd be willing to bet I could prove you had a hand with that attempted murder of the boy. I've got enough to hang you."

Conn laughed mockingly. "Matthew Bodine. City Marshal. Hell, you ain't nothing. You've got no jurisdiction outside the town. You can't touch me."

"Maybe. Maybe not. I'll be the one to worry about that. Doesn't make any difference to me. You're under arrest for the attempted murder of Tommy Brandom. Are you going to come along without any problem? Or are you going to make me take you in with force?"

"Pretty sure of yourself, are you, Bodine? You don't even have a gun in your hand. What makes you think you could outdraw me?"

"I know it. You do, too. Just unbuckle your gunbelt and drop it."

"You're as crazy as Petty, except maybe in a different way. Why risk your life to take me in?"

"Maybe you said it. Maybe I am crazy. Doesn't make any difference. Stop stalling."

Conn reached for his buckle, but at the last instant went for the gun. It cleared leather and he shot. The bullet went low. It whizzed past Matt and hit the ground behind him.

Matt's draw was a blur. He shot once with deadly accuracy. The slug hit Conn's cheek, blasted through bone, exited through the back of his head. His eyes suddenly went empty as his hand instinctively clutched at his face, blood spurting through his fingers. He fell, blood coating his arm and running down his shirt-front.

Sam was surprised to find Derrell so close to catching up with Petty. Sam could see Derrell's bloody clothes and knew he was hurt. He suddenly had a lot more respect for the other man. Derrell had more courage than Sam had realized.

Petty's horse splashed into the creek. Sam didn't shoot, afraid of hitting Lilly by mistake.

Derrell chased Petty into the creek and with his last strength reached out and grabbed Petty by the arm. The outlaw turned in disbelief and tried to push Derrell away. At the same time, Lilly punched out and twisted in the saddle, forcing Petty off balance. He started to fall. Sam now was able to catch up. He jumped off the horse on top of Petty, forcing him into the water.

Sam struck with a vicious right to Petty's midsection, followed by a left to the head. The outlaw, with a crazy look in his eyes, started to lash out wildly with blows to Sam's face and stomach. Sam blocked most of them, but a few managed to get through. The blows that hit sounded like a stick hitting against a side of beef.

Sam ducked underneath a particularly reckless blow and threw Petty into the water near a pile of brush.

Just a few feet away, Derrell was trying to help Lilly toward dry land, and yelled out.

"Snakes!"

The churning water had disturbed a nest of snakes in the brush, and they were swimming wildly toward

Derrell and Lilly. Derrell, though still in pain, pushed Lilly toward the shore and started to grab at the snakes. He threw the one in his hand as far downstream as he could, but there were too many of them. Several bit him. Lilly screamed and pulled them off Derrell as they both moved toward the shore.

Sam took a step toward the couple, but stopped when he heard Petty's laugh.

"Got you now, Two-Wolves. You're a dead man."

Sam, though knee-deep in water, turned with an amazing speed and saw the gun in Petty's hand. The outlaw cocked and started to pull the trigger.

Sam's draw was faster than it had ever been. The gun like magic was out of its holster and in his hand. He squeezed off a shot, hitting Petty in the shoulder, spinning him around. Petty shot, but the bullet went wild.

Sam fired again, this time hitting the outlaw squarely in the chest, knocking him back into the brush. Petty screamed as another set of snakes suddenly appeared and swarmed over him.

The blood brother rushed over to where Lilly and Derrell were almost to the creek bank. Sam helped pull the couple from the water. Several snakes were still trailing behind them. Sam killed them with well-placed shots. The water was again still, except for the floating bodies of the dead snakes and King Petty.

"Didn't leave much for me to do?" Matt asked as he rode up.

"I got to him first," Sam answered.

Lilly was crying as she kneeled over Derrell.

"Will he be all right?" Lilly asked, touching Derrell's face. "He risked his life to save me. Will he live?"

Sam looked him over, saw several red welts where the snakes had bitten. He took his knife and cut back the pants to take a better look at the bullet wound.

"He's not in good shape," Sam admitted. "But Derrell Brown is a strong man. And I have a friend in town that knows some old remedies that might help him. I'd lay odds that Derrell will pull through as strong as ever."

"Could you get your friend to help him? Please?"

"I'm already going," Matt said.

"Tell Clarissa we'll be at Lilly's place. She'll need to bring some of her special tea and dressings."

"Please save him, Clarissa. Don't let him die."

Lilly's voice was pleading as Clarissa put the palm of her hand against Derrell's forehead.

"The fever's going down. The poultices are working. The danger is past. He'll live."

"Thank you, Clarissa . . . thank you!"

Clarissa looked thoughtfully at the man stretched out in the bed. "It's not really my doing," she said. "Derrell has a strong will to live . . . he has a strong reason to live. And I think you know what it is."

"I . . . do know . . . but it's been so soon since . . . since . . ."

"The hurt will heal in time. Just let it heal. And accept the gift of love when it's offered."

Derrell groaned. Sam and Matt, sitting in the adjoining room, looked through the door.

"What he needs now is tender loving care. You look after him for a while."

As Clarissa left to join Matt and Sam, Lilly was

smoothing the covers around Derrell with a concerned look on her face.

"How is he?" Sam asked.

"The worst is over. The best is yet to come."

Chapter 22

Clarissa and Henry Ponder were behind the counter, restocking cans on shelves. Clarissa turned when Sam entered, smiled, and stepped down to greet him with a hug. Henry waved and called out, "Hi, Sam!"

"Henry. Clarissa. I came to tell you both goodbye."

"You done what you came for," Henry said, holding out his hand. "We were hoping you'd stop by before leaving."

"Well, that's not entirely true," Sam said, smiling. "Never did get that fishing out of my system."

"Too many snakes?" Henry asked.

"Too many snakes—of all kinds," Sam agreed. He leaned his hip against the counter. "We got rid of some of those critters, with your and Clarissa's help. It took a lot of courage to do what you did."

"We should have acted against Petty a long time ago, but we were all scared. Until you and Matt came along and stood up against him. Matt gave us a little scare when we thought he was going to turn down the offer to serve as marshal . . . but it worked out."

"Matt's a little hard-headed sometimes, especially

when his fishing is interrupted," Sam said. "But you can count on him. Always."

Clarissa laughed and suggested, "You two are very close."

"Closer than brothers," Sam agreed.

"I've got to run," Henry said. "A town council meeting scheduled, to fill the marshal job. Wish you and Matt would stay."

"Can't do it."

"I understand." Henry shook Sam's hand again and said, "You come up this way again. You're always welcome here. Maybe next time you'll even get that fishing done!"

Henry took off his apron and left through the rear door, leaving Clarissa and Sam in the room. The room was quiet, but not uncomfortable. Clarissa finally said, "You've been thinking about our talk?"

"Not much time to think, not with all that's been going on."

"Sam . . . that's an excuse. Not a reason."

Sam smiled. "You're a lot like my mother. You've seen through me." He paused, then said more seriously, "Have you wondered why I don't live my life as a Cheyenne? It's because a long time ago I made a promise to my father to turn my back on my life as an Indian. Of course, I sometimes have doubts. But I couldn't go back now."

"That's not what I said," Clarissa said. "I said to keep your heritage in your heart . . . recognize it . . . and live it. My grandmother was Cherokee, though nobody knows that but Henry and you. That's not important. What is important is that I know. And that I try to live the old ways in my heart. You should realize, if you don't already, that you *are* living as a Cheyenne . . . in your heart. You have the soul of a warrior. I know you still follow many of the Cheyenne ways. Most important, you are true to what you believe is right. That is the most important thing."

"Thanks, Clarissa."

"One more question."

"Sure. Anything."

"You and Sam are blood brothers, aren't you?"

"Yes."

"That explains a lot. Others, like Henry, accept us, but could not truly hope to understand." She hugged Sam. "Take care. You and Matt will always have a place here."

Derrell Brown was stretched out on one of the easy chairs in Lilly's front room, his legs bandaged and his face puffy from the bullet wound and the snake bites that he had received. He was a tough fellow, however, and had survived the nights and days following the bites, first with Clarissa's help and then with Lilly's. He would live.

Lilly stood near him, a concerned look on her face as she plumped his pillow and tried to make him comfortable.

Matt was on the front porch, enjoying the spring weather and watching Sam ride in from town. Sam's horse came to a sliding stop. He tied it to the porch rail and came up the stairs in one jump. He glanced through the open door, saw Lilly and Derrell talking to each other.

Matt looked at Sam and grinned.

"Looks like Lilly will come out of this all right."

"Her husband's death is still too recent; the loss is too fresh," Sam answered thoughtfully. "It does seem obvious that there is an attraction between those two."

"Derrell came near killing himself when he pulled the woman from the river. That's a bit more than just an attraction."

"It does make him seem like a hero to her," Sam said. "That Tommy likes him, and the feeling is mutual, doesn't hurt either."

"Lilly's an attractive woman. Aren't you a little jealous that you—Mr. Sam Two-Wolves, the ladies man—lost out this time to Derrell?"

Sam hit Matt with his hat, laughing softly.

Matt turned from the scene, walked to the edge of the porch, and looked across the fields.

"Sometimes I wish I had this wanderlust played out. That I could just find a woman and stay in one place for more than a few weeks at a time. Go home, and stay home."

"I know what you mean. Lilly and Derrell will have a good life here. The land is rich, there's plenty of water, it'll be a good place to raise kids. I can say the same about our ranches up north. But I'm wondering if that's what I really want. Is that really me? Is that really the life for me?"

Matt knew Sam better than anybody. Sometimes it was better not to joke. He said seriously, "You're thinking about your promise to your father to turn your back on your Indian heritage."

"Yeah. That's it. I did more than promise. I made a sacred oath. And I'll die before I renege on that oath. But something just doesn't seem right. Sometimes I feel I'm missing something, and don't know what. I'm not entirely comfortable with the new ways, but I couldn't go back to the old ways—even if I wanted to."

"You'll figure it out in time," Matt said. "Maybe a trip home would help."

"Maybe. It's something to think about."

Lester Brown came around the corner of the house, talking with Tommy as the boy led a cow pony. Tommy saw Matt and Sam and waved.

"Mr. Brown is telling me about being a cowboy!" Tommy said excitedly.

"Tommy?" Brown said.

"Sorry. Lester was telling me about cows and showing me a little about riding."

Derrell and Lilly heard the talk outside. Derrell hobbled to the door, leaning a little on Lilly. Lester said to the woman, "Just telling the boys about your son. He's a natural. If you don't mind, I'd like to have your boy help me and Derrell out some . . . and we'll help you on your place."

"That'd be . . . wonderful!" Lilly said.

"Then it's a done deal." Brown's bushy eyebrows cast shadows under his eyes as he turned to Matt and Sam. "Looks like you boys are headed out."

"Time to move on," Matt said.

"Wish you all could stay awhile."

"We'll make it back this way, I suspect," Sam said.

"Where to in the meantime?"

"Haven't decided yet," Matt said. "We may continue north . . . up to our home places. Or we may head to the southwest and see the desert country. Or we might wind up someplace totally different. Depends on which way the wind blows."

The two blood brothers stepped into their saddles, waved one final goodbye and then headed down the road. Soon, Lilly's house was out of sight.

"Been meaning to talk with you for a while," Matt said, a serious look on his face.

"So talk."

"I'm trying to figure out how one fellow can get himself in so much trouble! Send you to town for some groceries, and next thing you know we're facing a killer. Think maybe next time I'll go in myself for supplies!"

"That so? Whose idea was it that we go after some cattle rustlers . . . just as a matter of principle?"

"Well . . . a man's got to live according to his own principles," Matt said, watching Sam out of the corner of his eye. "Wouldn't you say . . . brother?"

Sam nodded. "You understand it well . . . brother."

Matt and Sam rode in silence for a while, enjoying the spring day. The two did not have to exchange words to communicate with each other, since they in fact did share a bond that would be impossible for most men to comprehend.

"So what's next?" Matt finally asked as the sun rose higher in the sky. "Want to head home for a while?"

"What's your thinking?"

"Well, I do have an idea."

"Not like you to be shy. Spit it out."

"I'd kind of like to head farther west."

"Any particular reason?"

"I've heard that there's some of those mountain streams that have some pretty good fishing . . ."

Matt howled and raced away. Sam laughed and gave chase with a loud rebel yell as the blood brothers hurried toward the next adventures waiting for them down the road in the West.